Relationship Status

Relationship Status

Deshon Dreamz

www.urbanbooks.net

Urban Books, LLC
300 Farmingdale Road, NY-Route 109
Farmingdale, NY 11735

Relationship Status

ISBN 13: 978-1-60162-913-5
ISBN 10: 1-60162-913-3

First Mass Market Printing June 2019
First Trade Paperback Printing August 2018
Printed in the United States of America

10 9 8 7 6 5 4 3 2 1

This is a work of fiction. Any references or similarities to actual events, real people, living or dead, or to real locales are intended to give the novel a sense of reality. Any similarity in other names, characters, places, and incidents is entirely coincidental.

Distributed by Kensington Publishing Corp.
Submit Orders to:
Customer Service
400 Hahn Road
Westminster, MD 21157-4627
Phone: 1-800-733-3000
Fax: 1-800-659-2436

Relationship Status

Deshon Dreamz

Chapter 1

Tori

One Year Ago

"It's freaking cold," I groaned as I walked down the street to my car. I called Keyton's phone for the twentieth time, just to have my call go straight to voicemail. I shook my head as I slid my phone back into my pocket. I was starting to wish I got dropped off. Texas weather was always crazy. I didn't know whether to wear a jacket or shorts. You just dressed neutral and prayed the temperature didn't drop. As I walked swiftly to the student parking garage, I smiled as I saw my car. I pushed the button to start the engine as I continued walking. I was so happy this day was over. I wrapped my jacket tighter around me and slid my hand over my stomach. I still remember the shock of finding out I was three months pregnant. Key was so excited, and so was I. I couldn't wait to meet our princess.

My steps slowed as an eerie feeling washed over me. I wondered where everyone was. We had exams coming up, so I knew I wasn't the only one who'd stayed late to study. It was so quiet. I quickened my pace to my car as the feeling grew heavier. When I finally made it, I exhaled and quickly opened the door to get in. *Thank God for push start and heated seats.*

As soon as I was in, I laid my head back on the headrest as I placed my bags in the passenger seat. I looked down at my ringing phone, rolling my eyes as I picked it up.

"About time you called back, Keyton! What the fuck was you doing that prevented you from answering the phone?"

"Where you at? School? Your parents'? Where are you?" The urgency in his voice sent chills down my spine. Goosebumps formed on my skin as fear crept into my heart.

"I'm at—"

Before I could complete my sentence, I was snatched out of my car. The scream I wanted to release got caught in my throat as I struggled against the strength of the person who grabbed me.

"Don't fight me, bitch. I'll break your fucking neck," he growled as he grabbed my hair, successfully pulled me completely out of the car, and threw me to the ground. "Beat the life out of this bitch," he announced.

I was too scared to look up, but I felt the presence of others. Before I could get a word out, I felt a blow to my face so hard that it knocked the wind out of me. I opened my eyes partially just to see the garage ceiling and four people dressed in all black. "Please don't! I'm pregnant!"

"Fuck you and that baby, bitch," the man spoke as I heard chains and bats click against the floor of the garage. "Fuck this bitch up!"

I couldn't describe the pain I felt from the blow of the bat against my arm. I cried out for Keyton in the fetal position, trying to protect my unborn child. The pain was unbearable. I could hear my bones cracking and the constant flow of blood from my head hitting the ground. I felt a sharp kick to my back then my stomach as I held her. I tried my best to protect her, but I couldn't. I just couldn't.

"Please stop," I screamed with all I had. "Keyton!"

"That bitch nigga can't save you! Fucking with bitch niggas get you put in bitch positions!"

"Somebody please help!" Blood leaked from my mouth and ears. I felt moisture between my legs, and I knew I was losing my baby. "Please, you're going to kill her! Please stop," I mumbled. "Keyton, help!"

My body went numb from pain as I gave up on ever seeing Keyton again. I gave up on life! I gave up on ever holding and kissing my daughter. He was my husband. Why wasn't he here to protect me?

"Pretty bitch ain't so pretty no more, huh?" one of my attackers spoke as she punched me in the face with brass knuckles repeatedly.

"Don't worry. I'll keep Keyton's dick wet while you gone, bitch!" The other one swung the bat against my stomach, crushing my hands in the process.

"That nigga doesn't give a fuck about you! Where he at?" the other spoke as she held me down.

The blows came to an abrupt stop as I shuddered on the floor. I was drifting in and out of consciousness as the world around me turned cold.

"You feel that, bitch?" the man taunted. "That's death! I'll see you when I make it to hell!"

I felt myself lose consciousness as moisture pooled between my legs. I knew it was blood, though I couldn't see it. I knew I had lost my daughter. I just needed to see her. I wanted to hold her and tell her that I loved her even though I allowed this to happen. She meant so much to me.

Chapter 2

Keyton

Present Day

"You only care about yourself! You're selfish and self-centered, and I hate you, Keyton!"

My hat was low, covering my eyes that were now red because I was dumb high. I was sitting on the couch in the downtown loft I shared with the love of my life, Tori Dior Miles. My estimate was that she had been yelling for the last thirty minutes. From what I gathered, because bitches be coming up with some shit, some chick from Facebook messaged Tori informing her that I knocked her down. That shit was a lie, but I couldn't get Tori to believe that. See, I fucked up in the past, and shit hadn't been right since, but

I wouldn't give up on us. I loved her too much. She was all I knew.

Man, this was my heart in front of me, my everything. She was about five feet six inches and chocolate with these pretty-ass light brown eyes. She looked exotic. The thing about Tori was that, though she was beautiful, she didn't have a conceited bone in her body. Speaking of her body, she had thick-ass curves for fucking days.

I liked to think I had something to do with that. She had deep dimples and a perfect smile, and she rocked a piercing in her bottom lip that only added to her beauty. She wore her hair bone straight, falling to the middle of her back, all hers.

I dared a nigga to touch my rib. I was fucking shit up on sight. The only issues we had was outside bitches dropping bugs in her ear and that she didn't trust me as far as she could see me.

We'd been rocking since high school, eight years to be exact, married for five. I locked her ass down as soon as we were legally able to do so. It took a minute to convince her father, but he eventually gave me his consent. He still thought we were too young to be married, though.

Been through some shit, but I wasn't messing up home for nobody. Tori was wifey! Point blank period. Even when her ass was flipping out on a nigga, like right now.

"You hate me, baby?" I laughed. I had to do something to keep from snatching her li'l ass up. "You say that every day! I don't want to hear that shit, ma."

Tori was in my face in seconds. *Sexy ass.* Even when she was spazzing on me, I couldn't help but smile because I loved her and all her craziness. She had this sexy little Boston accent, too. I don't know, man. I was crazy about this girl. She could do no wrong in my eyes. Before I knew it, she had hauled off and hit my ass dead in the chest. I had to grab my shit. She was a little violent. Shit stung.

"I don't see anything funny!"

I was still rubbing my chest where she hit me. "Say, Tor. Keep your hands to yourself!"

"Fuck you, Keyton! I do hate yo' dog ass! All you do is lie and cheat! Bitches are calling my phone! You even got chicks at my school wanting to fight me and shit all because my nigga can't keep his dick in his pants! Fuck you!" she screamed at my ass.

Tori grabbed her Coach purse from the chair in the dining room and her keys off the table. We always argued, but she only tried to leave me twice before. My heart dropped to my fucking feet.

The fuck? My high evaporated. I was thrown off. At first, I didn't know whether I was supposed to stop her or let her leave. She was tired. I could see it, but I couldn't let her just leave over no bullshit another chick said. I loved her too much. Eight years of loving her and I wasn't letting her go. I accepted my past fuckups, but this shit here wasn't on me.

In all the years I'd been with shorty, I fucked her over once with one of the strippers at the club. Then, I didn't even have sex with her. I just let her suck my dick. I knew it was wrong and was planning on telling Tori and dealing with the consequences, until the chick approached her one night at the club, talking about how we fucked in my office. It took everything I had to get Tori back after that.

She moved out, took all her shit, and changed her number. I tell you, a nigga was sick! I couldn't eat, couldn't sleep. I stalked her ass and begged more than a Keith Sweat greatest hits collection until I got her back. I wasn't losing her again.

She was almost to the door when I stepped in front of her. I was trying to have a chill night, but I had to deal with this shit.

"Aye, Tor, how many times I got to tell yo' spoiled ass you ain't leaving shit? We locked the fuck in, so put that shit down."

"Move out my way, Keyton. I'm not doing this anymore. I'm not beat for it. Eight years and you ain't got your shit together yet? I'm done."

Tori wiped the tears that gathered in her eyes before she returned her gaze to mine. This was fucking with me mentally. The thought of her leaving had me sick to my stomach. I still loved Tori with all of my heart, but I knew things had not been the same between us since that shit went down. I felt like I was losing her.

"You are blowing my high, man."

"You ruining your own shit. Just let me leave!"

"Fuck nah! Put that down! You all I fucking got! I'm not about to let you just leave because of what some chick said! I come home expecting to get sexed to sleep, but no, I walk into this shit. Some bitch said this, some bitch said that, some bitch told you I was fucking the next bitch. Word-of-mouth-ass hoes. You just eat all that shit up! I'm tired of this same shit, Tori!"

She mushed my ass so hard I had to bite into my bottom lip to control my reaction.

"Say! Watch yo' hands, baby girl," I said, licking my lips again. "Don't touch me unless we fucking. Are we fucking or nah?"

"It's a million females in Dallas willing to have yo' dog ass! Go fuck one of them!"

I was stressed. "Damn, Tori! You my wife! I don't want any of them girls, man. Come on now. My dick hard, and yo' sexy ass yelling in my face ain't making it no better. I wanna fuck!"

"That's your problem, Keyton. That's all you ever want to do. Run the streets, get high, and fuck!"

I shook my head. "This shit for the birds, man."

We stood there for a moment, neither of us speaking to each other, just looking deep into the other's eyes. Tori probably didn't realize she was crying again until I reached out and wiped her cheek. I looked down at my hand. Her tears were like my biggest enemy. Seeing those shits was worse than facing my haters in the streets. I would have rather gone to war with a foe than see her cry.

"Stop that, man. I can't take it. I ain't messing around on you, Tori. I messed up in the past, but that was the old me. I love you, ma. A nigga got flaws, I ain't gon' front, but the girls out there can miss me with that shit. I ain't fucking up home for no one-time smash. Not again. Not anymore."

She tried to wipe her face, but the more she swiped, the more tears came falling from her eyes and into my heart.

"You say things like that then do something different. I'm not a fool, Keyton. I know I can't believe everything that comes out of these women's mouths, but what the hell, Key? I deal with so much already with you not being here all the time. You have the restaurants and the club. Now you working on the hotel. You're rarely here! I'm always by myself or with Nia. I'm your wife, Keyton."

"I know that, Tori!"

"Then act like it!" she yelled as she got closer to me. "Keyton, can't you see I'm tired of this shit? It's not just these females coming out of nowhere! It's this marriage! It's the fact that I don't get to make love to my husband every night because he always has other shit to tend to! If you were here with me, I could have some kind of defense against all this, but when a bitch tells me she had my dick, I can't even say, 'No, bitch, because I had that motherfucker last night!' I can't because that would be a lie!"

I didn't have shit to say because she was right. Everything she was saying was right, and I couldn't deny that. I couldn't say a thing.

"Tori, you know I love you, and I don't want to lose you. Just give me a chance to get some shit together. I'll be home more, I promise!"

"Fuck your promises, Key. Keep that! I'm starting to believe you just make promises to me to break them. Because they sound good, right?"

I was beyond pissed off at this point. I knew there was a lot of shit that Tori wasn't saying. I knew what the real issue was, but if she didn't bring it up, then neither would I. "Man, what the fuck you want from me?"

"I don't want anything from you, Keyton! Not shit!"

I exhaled as I ran my hands down my face. "So what are we doing, Tori?"

She sniffed and wiped her eyes again. "I'm leaving!"

"No, you not! So what other options do we have?" I sounded like a bitch, but I didn't give a fuck. I was in the wrong even though I hadn't done anything wrong. I didn't even know the woman she was talking about. I could admit I hadn't been around lately, but I was trying to put some things in place for us. I wanted Tori to always be good with or without me.

"Do you still want to have my daughter? Do you even still love me? You're my wife, been that for five years. Do you still want to be married to me? Do you give a fuck at all, man?" I asked as I looked into her eyes.

"I love you, Keyton. You know that!"

"I hear you say it all the time, but I can't feel it, Tori. Not since—"

She looked at me sharply. "Not since what? Say it!"

I held my head down. *Fuck!* My intentions weren't to bring that shit up, but I knew that was our problem. When she lost our daughter, she changed. The woman I fell in love with was no longer there behind her beautiful eyes. Everything was just blank. Gone. Empty. I loved my wife with every inch of me, but things between us just hadn't been the same. "I'm not going there."

She bit her bottom lip and stared at me. "Since what, Key?"

"Come on, Tori."

"Fucking say it," she cried, pushing me in the chest. I tried to grab her, and she snatched away from me.

"I just know you don't love me the same," I said, shaking my head.

She ran her hands through her hair and shook her head. "I need you to let me go."

"I just told you I can't do that, ma."

"But that's not your choice to make, Keyton. I'm leaving."

"So what that mean, Tori? I asked you if you wanted to keep being my wife. I asked you if you wanted to try again to have the little girl you keep asking me for. I wanna know. Tell me!"

"I can't live like this, Keyton. I can't!"

I couldn't remember the last time I shed tears, but I felt as if I was on the verge of letting some go now. "But, ma . . . You can't leave me, Tori. You all I fucking got, man. What I'm supposed to do if you ain't here? Who do I kiss? Make love to? Who gon' hold Key down?"

She bowed her head. "Please, Key, just let me go."

I took a few steps closer to her. "Let you go?" I was disgusted with her for saying some shit like that! "And do what? You got a plan, right? You know everything? Let you go. Then what? What a nigga gon' do without his heart and soul, Tori? You might as well take that cute-ass Bedazzled nine you got in your purse and kill a nigga, because that's the only thing you leaving gon' do."

She looked up at me as fresh tears gathered in her eyes. I walked into her and wrapped my arms around her waist, pulling her into me. Soft whimpers came from her lips as she cried harder. I buried my face in her neck and inhaled deeply.

"Why shit gotta be so hard, Keyton?" she asked through her sobs.

"I'm sorry, Tori. I'm trying to make it right, but you gotta give me a chance. I'll do whatever I gotta do, ma. I can't lose you." I planted kisses on her neck and shoulders as I held her. I needed this woman. I knew it, and so did she.

Chapter 3

Tori

I knew this was a losing battle. He wasn't going to let me leave. I mean, what Keyton didn't get was that we wouldn't be having this conversation if the chick who stated they messed around just last weekend hadn't messaged me on Facebook. Apparently, they got a room after the club and fucked around. He hadn't made it home until four that morning, so it could possibly be true.

I met Keyton Miles when I moved to Dallas from Boston when I was in the tenth grade. My father was offered a job opportunity that required leaving our hometown. He had since taken over that company and renamed it, and he was now the active CEO of Jones Construction.

The moment I laid eyes on Keyton, I instantly fell in love with him. He was a grade ahead of me, so most of the time I admired him from afar. He was the jock of the school, into all the sports. I was just the nerdy new girl with the weird accent. The only time I saw him was early in the morning, passing in the hallway, or when school was let out. I had the biggest crush on him.

He was six feet three inches, with mocha skin and the most beautiful dark marble eyes. His presence threw me off, made me lose focus on anything outside of him. He worked out, so his body was right. He had a bold, solid frame and a well-defined six pack. He was extremely attractive, and over the years that attraction only multiplied. He had tattoos that covered most of his chest, with my name tatted on his neck. He kept his hair cut low with deep waves, and he had a goatee. I was most attracted to his lips, though: thick, soft, and pink. I literally licked them every chance I got. He was just everything I wanted in a man. I remembered the day I was bold enough to speak. I was fucking weird, now that I thought about it.

Sophomore year, I was rushing out of home-room, trying to meet up with my best friend, Nia. When I turned the corner, I ran into a hard chest, causing my books to hit the floor before my ass did.

"Damn, ma. You a'ight?"

I was so embarrassed. I didn't even look up to see who I collided with. The hall was super crowded, and I even heard a few people laugh. For some reason, they didn't laugh long, though. I started to pick up my books and papers that hit the floor, and the person I ran into bent down to help.

"My bad, baby girl. I ain't see you."

I tried not to be affected by his voice, but it was so perfect. It was one of those nighttime voices. The ones you want talking to you as you fall asleep. I wondered what Keyton sounded like up close.

"It's okay," I whispered as I hurriedly stuffed my books into my backpack. I reached for my chemistry book at the same time he did, so I quickly let it go. I then stood and looked into the face of the person I almost tackled.

"You shouldn't run, Tori. It's against the rules," he said, handing me the book.

My mouth went dry. Palms sweaty. I nervously ran a hand through my hair before grabbing the book from him. It was him, Keyton Miles, and he knew my name. I fought hard to control my breathing.

"I . . . You . . . I didn't see you. I'm sorry," I stuttered like a three-year-old trying to get a sentence out.

He just smiled at me, showing perfect white teeth. "It's all right. So, where you rushing to?"

I looked down. I didn't understand why I was acting like I'd never been in the presence of a boy before. "I have to meet TaNia."

"Your friend Nia?"

I frowned. How did he know so much about me? TaNia was quiet and kept to herself, so I didn't know he knew of her.

He smiled at me again, and I thought I would melt into the ground. "Can I walk you?"

I fought the urge to look around to see if anyone was behind me. Surely, he wasn't talking to my ass.

"Aye, Key?"

I turned to see Lemonte, Keyton's best friend, calling him.

"Leave Tori alone and come on, man. You already knocked her over. She ain't tryin'a hear that weak crap you spitting." He shook his head, laughing. "Coach said you got five minutes or that's twenty suicides. I ain't tryin'a be late wit'cho ass."

"Bro, I'm coming!"

"Aye, Tori, tell thick-ass Nia the kid said what's up!" Mon yelled before he walked off, laughing.

I shook my head. Nia stayed curving Mon, but he wouldn't give up. He was super handsome, so I never understood why Nia wouldn't give him the time of day.

"Will you save that walk for me? I ain't tryin'a do suicides today."

I looked up at him, smiling as I nodded. "Yes."

Key smiled. "All right, beautiful. Stay good and watch where you going. I ain't tryin'a have you bumping into everybody."

I walked off from him on cloud nine. I couldn't wait to get to Nia and tell her what happened. Only my best friend knew my feelings for Keyton.

Now, eight years later, I still loved him the same, but it was tainted love due to all the hurt and stress. Being with Keyton had brought me so much joy, just not enough to overshadow all the pain.

"Can you just let me go, Key?"

He released me but pressed his body softly into mine so I couldn't move. He took his hat off and threw it on the table. "That's what you want?" he asked as he removed his hoodie. "All these years down the drain over this shit? Nah, baby girl, I can't rock with that."

I made a move to go around him, only to have the front of me pushed against the door. "Stop, Key."

He pressed his dick against my ass. This motherfucker didn't play fair. "You really gon' leave me, Tori?"

I heard the hurt in his voice. Just the thought of me leaving him was messing his head up. It was messing my head up too, but it's what I needed.

The thing was I didn't understand Key. He entertained all these chicks and expected me to just stay down and accept it. How do you handle a different female a week while yelling bullshit about the love of your life? I couldn't fade it. I was done. At least I wanted to be.

I grabbed the doorknob to open the door. "I'm tired of coming in second place behind these bitches."

Keyton reached around me and pushed the door closed. "You ain't second to shit. I've loved you since I was in the eleventh grade. That ain't gon' change."

"I come second to everything! I hate the day you opened that fucking club! Since then it's been nothing but bullshit!"

Key, Mon, and Marco owned one of the most popular strip clubs in Dallas. Club Pure was packed six nights a week. Anybody who was somebody was there every Saturday night. I didn't club often. I was too busy working on my master's degree in journalism and mass communication, but when I did step out, Club Pure was always the destination. I kid you not, every time I stepped in that muthafucka, there was a hating bitch, spilling drinks "accidentally" and claiming they knew how my man's dick tasted. All kinds of shit! I always had to correct some females for barking hot shit. It would be so different if I trusted Key. I could tell a female to get up out my face with no hesitation, but he fucked that up when he cheated on me with that stripper. I knew what came along with loving Key. I just wished it were different. On top of the club, he also had a few restaurants he ran with his two friends. They were young, but they were known in Dallas for being businessmen.

"Want me to close that mutherfucka down? Just say it. I'll do it."

I felt his hand come down to caress my scalp. He knew everything about me, all of my likes and dislikes. He knew playing in my hair or massaging my scalp was a weakness.

"Where you going? Yo' mom's crib? Over there with Nia?" He brought his other hand down to caress my ass. Second weakness. I didn't want to moan but found myself doing so anyway.

"All I'm gon' do is find what's mine and put it back in its rightful place."

I felt his hand slip past the waistband of my shorts and caress my pussy through my panties. He began to kiss my neck and earlobe, making me even wetter. His finger slid between my folds as his fingertips moved over my clit. I pressed my forehead to the door and bit my bottom lip. All that hot shit I was just talking flew out the window.

My moans turned into whimpers as his fingers moved inside of me. I felt weak in the knees, lightheaded. "Keyton," I moaned out as he removed his hand from my pants and turned me around. Before I could protest, he was on his knees in front of me, removing my shorts and panties.

"Then you want me to let you give my pussy away?" he said as he lifted one of my legs onto his shoulders with my back still against the door.

He planted a kiss on each thigh, softly biting me there before he French kissed my clit.

I thought I would fall, but he held me steady up against the door. He was the only man to ever touch me in this manner, and everything he did to me brought me to orgasms quick.

When I felt his tongue enter me, I bucked against the door and grabbed his shoulder. Given that I didn't have anyone to compare him to, I couldn't really say he had the best head, but shit, I doubted anyone was fucking with him in the oral sex department. Shit, sex period.

In a matter of minutes, my thighs were shaking. "Keyton, please," I half moaned and half screamed as my body convulsed. He locked down on my clit, flicking his tongue slowly against it, only intensifying my orgasm. "Ohhhhhhh shit, Keyyyyy!"

My screams bounced off the walls as I came. My eyes rolled to the back of my head as he stood with me in his arms and made his way to the bedroom. He tossed me on the bed. I liked that rough shit.

"You want to leave?" he asked, eyes glazed over. He removed his belt from the loops and removed his clothes. For a moment, I just looked at him. I was still coming down from my orgasm, incoherent.

"You still want to leave me? Huh?" he said as he got in bed with me, quickly removing the rest of my clothes. I watched in amazement as all eleven inches of him stood at attention. Not only was it long, it was thick. I had a hard time handling it still, even after all these years of fucking. "You ain't gon' answer?"

He placed my knees on his arms and pushed my legs up until my ankles were by my ears. It was this moment when I knew I fucked up.

He slapped my clit with his dick, causing my body to jerk before he placed the head inside me.

"Shit," I moaned out as he continued to give himself to me slowly. "Fuck, Keyton."

"You gon' leave?" He went as deep inside of me as he could before he moved back out. The sound of sex echoed in the room. He had my ass wide open already. "Damn, Tori."

He began digging deep into me. All I could do was push him back with my hands and scream with every stroke. He let my legs go to push my hand back, and he continued to fuck me long and deep. He looked me in my eyes the whole time as if he weren't fucking the life out of me. I squeezed my eyes shut as he went deeper. I planted my hand on his abs again to stop him from going deeper, and he popped my ass like I was a kid caught with my hand in the cookie jar.

"Move yo' fucking hands. Take this shit. It belongs to you!"

My body tensed up as another orgasm sneaked up on me. "Keyton, I'm cumming. Ohhh, fuck!"

"Yeaaaah," he boasted. He took his dick out and slapped my clit, causing me to squirt all over his stomach. "Didn't I tell you you come first?" He licked his lips. "Give my dick what he deserves. Cum on that shit!"

My ass almost blacked out, but he didn't stop. He flipped me over, pinning me to the bed with his hands as he entered me from the back. I moved forward when he was as deep as he could go.

He hit me on the ass hard, causing me to scream out.

"Don't run from shit. You hear me? Don't make me hold yo' ass down!"

"Okay," I pleaded with him. "I won't run, I promise."

"Keep that ass up." His hand came around to massage my clit. "Keep yo' head down like you dodging shit." He chuckled. He was still high, but I was giving his ass a different high altogether.

He reentered me, and I almost came instantly. Between his fingers on my clit and his dick entering me at such a pace, I was on cloud nine.

I felt intoxicated. Drunk. He sped up inside of me, and I felt myself cream all over him.

"Look at that shit. You think I'm 'bout to give this good shit up over some bullshit? You belong to me," he groaned as he continued to drill me. I felt drained and dizzy. I wanted to speak but I couldn't. My eyes watered as he continued hitting my spot.

"Tell me this pussy belongs to me, Tor! Talk to daddy!"

I bit my lip. "It's yours! Ohhh damn, baby. It's yours, Keyton!"

"This mines!" he stated as he smacked my ass. "This shit so fucking good!" He grabbed a handful of my hair as he brought me up to him. "You gon' leave?"

I didn't know what to do or say. All I knew was I was on the verge of another orgasm, and I didn't want him to stop. "Please, Keyton. I'm about to come! Don't stop, daddy!"

He slowed his pace. "You want me to take this shit out?"

I quickly whispered the word no.

"Answer me!" he said as he continued to slowly grind into me, still hitting my spot just at a slower pace. The shit was torture.

"I'ma stay!" I screamed before I knew it. "I'm not going nowhere, baby! Please just fuck me!" Shit, I'd tell his ass anything.

He pulled his dick out completely and flipped me over. I was about to protest when he lifted my legs up and placed them on his shoulders. He then put his fingers in my mouth. Removing them, he placed two of them inside me. He looked directly into my eyes as he moved his fingers in a "come here" motion inside of my wetness, causing my thighs to shake. "I don't wanna hear shit about you leaving me! You can't leave a nigga, Tor. I couldn't stomach that shit! I couldn't handle it, baby girl! You hear me?"

"Yessssss, daddy. Oh fuckkk!"

He removed his fingers and placed them back inside of my mouth, allowing me to taste myself as he bent down and ran his tongue over my clit. "So fucking good," I heard him groan as his tongue lapped over my whole vagina. I was ready to tap the fuck out. I grabbed the sheets to keep from scratching him up, and I bit the hell out of my bottom lip to keep from screaming.

"Damn, Keyton! Please don't stop."

I then moaned something I didn't understand. He was sexing me like he was pissed off and pleasure was my punishment.

He withdrew his tongue from me as he pushed my legs farther back again to enter me quickly. He had my legs pushed back so far that our faces were inches apart.

"Say you're sorry, ma," he moaned in my ear. "You almost broke a nigga heart, man. You can't say that shit to me."

"I'm sorry, daddy! I'm so fucking sorry," I moaned, squeezing my eyes shut.

"You didn't mean that shit, did you?" He moved inside me, hitting spots I didn't know I had.

"No! I didn't mean it! I promise you, I didn't mean it," I cried out. "I'm coming, Keyton."

"My Tori," he mumbled close to my ear as he continued to give me long, deep strokes that had a bitch borderline hyperventilating.

I mumbled something back, but I didn't know what the fuck I was talking about.

"What was that?" his cocky ass had the nerve to ask. "Enunciate that shit, Tor."

He flipped me on my side and entered me, going deep as fuck. I was incoherent at this point. I was there physically, but mentally I was somewhere else. I couldn't process a thought. All I could do was feel. This was Key's form of punishment: fucking me into submission. I felt his body tense, and I knew he was about to cum. I clamped my vaginal muscles down on his dick like a vise grip. "Oh shit, Tori!"

He came long and hard inside of me, slowly collapsing behind me. "Fuck, Tori!"

He smacked my ass and pulled my motionless body closer to him. I was exhausted. I couldn't feel my legs, and attempting to protest would just leave me in more trouble. So, I snuggled next to him as we both drifted off to sleep.

Chapter 4

TaNia

I can't fit in this dress. I look fat. Shit, I am fat. This was nothing new, but I was gorgeous! I didn't lack confidence at all, but sometimes I had these moments. I always did every time I spent more than ten minutes in a mirror. I let the dress drop to the floor, as I looked at myself in my nude-colored matching panty and bra set. My thighs were the biggest things on me. My ass came in a strong second. I was always big. Not once had I ever been in a single-digit dress size. In high school, I was a ten, and now at twenty-five, I was a solid twelve or fourteen.

I carried my size well, though. I wasn't sloppy and hanging all over the place. I always kept my hygiene up. Nails, toes, and hair done. Right now, I rocked Havana Twist. My smooth caramel skin glistened from the coconut oil that I applied fresh out of the shower. I licked then puckered my lips as I examined my face: chestnut eyes, perfectly arched eyebrows, thick, full lips, high cheekbones, and an oval face. I was always told that I was pretty for a big girl.

But, I didn't want to be pretty for a big girl. I wanted to be seen as beautiful, period. Most times I did, I had my father to thank for that. There wasn't a morning when I didn't receive a compliment from him. From the time I was about five up until the day he passed away, he would tell me, "TaNia, you are the second most beautiful girl in the world, your mother being first!" I loved to hear him say that to me. I missed him every second!

I hated when I got in these moods where I downed myself because of the way that I looked. I didn't always feel unattractive. Most days I woke up feeling beautiful, like the queen I was, ready to tackle the day. Today wasn't one of those days. I didn't think that having a day where I felt unpretty and unhappy as a thicker woman meant having low self-esteem. I thought everyone was entitled to a moment of self-evaluation. This was just my moment.

I heard my phone ring. Figuring it was my best friend, Tori, I picked up. "What's up, girly?"

"Hello, beautiful!" a male's voice answered instead.

I rolled my eyes. I definitely wasn't in the mood for Mon. I still wanted to kill Tori for giving him my number. "What's up, Lemonte? What can I do for you?" I wasn't even trying to hide my attitude.

"You always so mean to me, beautiful. What I ever do to you?"

"You haven't done anything. I'm just not sure why you insist on calling me."

He laughed this sexy-ass laugh that made my heart jump. "You got a fly-ass mouth."

"What's up, Mon?" I asked, attempting to make this conversation short.

He laughed. "I got the antidote for that shit, though."

I exhaled deeply and rolled my eyes.

"Yeah, all that," he said, still laughing. "But I'm in your neck of the woods."

I rolled my eyes again. "Was there a purpose for your call?"

"Same purpose. I have been stalking yo' ass since high school, ma. I ain't giving up on making you mines, so you might as well get with this shit."

I couldn't do anything but laugh. I wouldn't lie to myself and say I wasn't attracted to Lemonte Reed. The motherfucker was beyond fine. That was the main reason I never took him seriously. He was perfect. Standing at six feet three inches, he had a perfect body, perfect pearly white teeth, and the most perfect smooth caramel skin. He had the prettiest light brown eyes and the nicest smile I'd seen. His dreads touched his upper back and shoulders, and he had tattoos covering his entire body. I always wanted to be with him, but I could never bring myself to do it. It was easier to be mean to him than to like him. It sounded childish, but even at my age, I had a lot of men play with my heart. I wouldn't let him be one of them. Letting my guard down to him would surely destroy me. I wasn't made to withstand a man like Lemonte.

"Look, man, she laughs," Mon said, talking to someone in the background.

My eyes got big. "You got me on speaker?"

"No, don't play me to the left like that. TaNia, I'm tryin'a kick it with you."

Damn, he made my name sound so fucking sexy. I looked at myself sideways in the mirror. I let my eyes slide over my body. My skin was so smooth and blemish free, and my curves were very well defined. I was bad as hell. *See, here I go with that up-and-down shit.*

"Why?"

"Why what?"

I ran my hands over my pudgy stomach, all in my thoughts and my feelings. What other purpose would I have with a dude like Mon outside of fucking and tossing me to the next nigga?

"Why me?" The insecurity in my voice was apparent, though I tried to cover it up.

"Shit, why not you would be a better question," he chuckled. "Who else? You're fucking beautiful, Nia. On top of that, you smart as shit, you have goals in life, plus you have a heart of gold. I'm trying to prove to you that I'm at least worthy of a shot with you."

I couldn't bring myself to believe anything he said to me. After all, he was "fine-ass hood nigga Lemonte Deon Reed," and I was "pretty for a fat girl TaNia Monae Jackson."

"A shot with me? Come on, Mon, all these women in Dallas, what you want me for?"

"Give me a chance to show you what I want." His voice was so fucking sexy. I had to get off this phone.

"I have to go, Mon."

"Why, Nia?"

"I have to get ready for class. I have to be there in an hour and fifteen minutes."

"Let me drop you off."

"Ummm, I have a car."

"I know that, TaNia. I'll be there in ten minutes. We can grab something to eat before."

"And what if I say no?"

"I say have yo' beautiful ass ready in ten minutes," he said before he hung up the phone.

This insane level of nervousness washed over me. I was going on a date with Lemonte. Why was I calling it a date? He never said date. But still, it was Lemonte! I had no idea what to do with myself! I looked at the phone for a moment before I poked my lips out and leaned my head back. I called the only person I could think of.

"Hey, girl! What's up?" Tori answered.

"Lemonte asked me out!" I screamed, just wanting to get it out.

"What?" she screamed back. "And you didn't say no?"

I rubbed my forehead. "He wasn't taking no for an answer! He just told me he would be here in ten minutes!"

"Oh, Lord! My baby going on a date," Tori said dramatically. "I should come take pictures!" She was fake crying at this point.

"Trick!" I said, annoyed. "I'm kind of losing my mind here!"

"For what? You are in love with that man. Go on the date!"

"I'm not in love with him," I mumbled.

"Girl, yes, the hell you are! You have been for the longest. He tired of you turning him down. Now, what are you wearing?"

I frowned. "I'm not dressing up. I have class right after. In fact, he's dropping me off."

Tori giggled. "Does that mean he's picking you up from class as well?"

I sat on the edge of my bed. "Shit, girl! I didn't even think of that!"

At that moment, a text came through from Mon.

Lemonte: I'm picking you up once you get out of class.

I looked at my phone for a minute before returning to Tori.

"Are you in the same room with him?"

"No, bitch, I'm at school! Why you ask that?"

I exhaled. "He just texted me and said he's picking me up once I get out of class."

Tori giggled. "I can't believe he finally got you!"

I became self-conscious. "What if I'm not the women he has been chasing all these years? I sure in hell ain't the same size I was when we were in high school."

"TaNia Monae," Tori said, taking on a more serious tone, "you are the most beautiful person I know, both inside and out. I think Mon sees that and doesn't want to be the idiot who lets you just walk into his life and not have you."

"That was sweet of you to say, Tori."

"Shit, if I were a man, I'd lock yo' ass down too! Hit it every time I got a chance to! Fuckkk you mean!"

I fell back on my bed, laughing. "I can't deal with you! Bye!" I hung up in her face. I loved Tori. I could always depend on her for whatever I needed, whether it was a good laugh, a shoulder to cry on, or anything and whatever. She was always there for me. I was that same friend to her.

I took a deep, calming breath before I threw my phone on the bed. I heard what Tori said, and I wanted so much to believe that I was the person she saw when she looked at me, but I wasn't. She was my friend, and I loved her, so just like she was the most beautiful woman to me, I was the most beautiful woman to her. Didn't mean Mon felt that way.

"Don't let him in, Nia. Don't let anyone in. All they want to do is hurt you," I said as I made my way to the closet.

Thinking this way was miserable for me, but it was a safe place I wasn't ready to leave just yet. I knew he would be here when he said, so I decided to go ahead and finish getting dressed. I grabbed my loose, ripped jeans and my tank top off my bed and walked into the bathroom. My appearance was everything. I didn't dress up for anyone but myself. I wanted to always look on point even if I didn't feel that way. My jeans hugged my thighs and hips, and my tank showed the slopes in my body. I decided to wear my all-black Retro 6's. I didn't feel like doing too much, so I applied natural-looking makeup and threw on some gold accessories.

When I walked out of my room, I found my mother in the kitchen. "Hey, Ma," I said, sitting at the table.

Diane Jackson was everything to me! I loved my mother more than anything in the world, and I always tried to be the best daughter to her. I didn't want my mom to feel lonely or think she didn't have anyone who loved her. That was far from the truth. For some reason, my mom liked Mon. She didn't know who he really was, though. If she did, she would have second thoughts.

"Hey, baby! How was work?"

"Busy." I worked overnight at the hospital as a receptionist. I was in school working on my bachelor's degree in forensics. I wanted to work for the FBI. "I'm so tired, but I have class."

"I don't know why you insist on working overnight, Nia. You have too much on your plate, honey."

"I know, Ma."

My mother looked at me for a long moment. All I wanted to do was be successful. My mother was young when she had me. She knew how life could pass you by if you didn't enjoy every day to the fullest. After losing her husband, my father, two years ago to prostate cancer, my mother knew she needed to enjoy every God-given moment, and she was going to be sure I did the same. Once my dad passed away, I immediately broke the lease to my apartment and moved back home. There was no way I was going to allow my mother to stay in this big house by herself.

"This job was supposed to be temporary. You don't have to work and you know that."

I grabbed an orange from the fruit bowl in the middle of the table and began peeling it, avoiding eye contact with my mother.

"So, when are you quitting, Nia?"

I got up to throw the orange peels in the trash. "I'm not," I mumbled under my breath. I sat back down like everything was normal.

"Excuse me?" My mother sat at the table with me. "We had a deal. After your dad died, you said you would work a little bit then quit. You're about to graduate college and move back into your own place. You need to focus."

"You sound like you don't want me here, Ma."

She shook her head as she stood to wipe the cabinet down. "I should sound like a mother who doesn't want her daughter left here alone."

I scrunched up my face and shook my head. "What are you talking about?" I hated when she talked like this. It made me feel like she was hiding something from me, and I didn't need any more surprises. Dad didn't let me know he was sick until he was dying, and I couldn't go through that again.

"I'm just saying, TaNia. Think about your future and not just mine."

I became irritated at the way she was beating around the bush. "When was the last time you went to the doctor, Momma?"

"See?" my mother said, stopping what she was doing to turn and look at me. "That's exactly the issue, TaNia Monae!"

I shrugged my shoulders. "What I do?"

"When was the last time *you* went to the doctor, TaNia?" I could tell she had an attitude, and that was a very good question.

I smirked as I replied. "I went to the doctor last night," I said, referring to my job.

"Don't make me pop you, little girl," my mother said, shaking her finger at me.

"Maaaaa," I groaned.

"Don't Maaaaa me! Answer my question!"

I started to think hard about her question. I hadn't been to the doctor since Dad passed. I definitely needed to make an appointment. "I'll make an appointment!"

"Don't give me attitude! You shouldn't dish out what you can't take!"

I shook my head, looking at her. "So, me being concerned about you is me giving you attitude?"

She placed her hands on her hips as she looked at me. "I don't need you to babysit me!"

I was shocked. I didn't know what to think or why I was on the verge of tears, but hearing her say those words shocked me. "I'm not here to babysit you, Ma. I don't want you out here alone! I'm just trying to be a good daughter to you!"

"While forgetting about you, TaNia," she stressed.

"How am I forgetting about myself?"

"When was the last time you bought yourself something or took yourself out? Went on a date? All you do is smother me, go to work, and go to school. It's a never-ending cycle, and I don't like seeing you caught in it!"

"Work won't be forever," I mumbled.

"I know that, because you are quitting! You will take time for yourself, TaNia. You only get one shot at this thing called life, and I won't watch you waste it!"

I popped an orange slice into my mouth and nodded. There was no point in debating with her, especially since she was right. "I know, Ma."

"I'll give you one more month, then you're quitting." My mother stepped away from the counter and resumed washing dishes.

"Ma, a month? That's barely enough time to put in my notice. Can you please give me two months? Three?"

"Nia, one month."

I knew not to push it with my mother. She was sweet, but she didn't play.

"When you going to get a boyfriend, Nia? You getting older and I want grandbabies."

I waved my hands. "Oh no. We are not going there, Ma! You'll get grandbabies once I'm married, and I'm only twenty-five. Don't start with the boyfriend thing, because I already know who you talking about and I don't want to sit through another Lemonte lecture."

My mother shrugged her shoulders. "Lemonte is nice."

"Pleasssseeeee, Ma!"

"All right, all right!" my mother said in surrender. She walked over to me, drying her hands on a napkin. "Honey, you're too young and beautiful to be hovering over me and working yourself to a pulp. I know that's what you're doing. I took losing your dad very hard. He was the love of my life! But I'm all right, I promise."

"I know, Momma," I said in a little-girl voice. "I just want to make sure that you're always all right. With Daddy gone it's just us now."

"I know, but I'm supposed to take care of you. Not the other way around."

I was about to respond when I heard a knock at the door. I picked up my phone and read the time. Ten minutes exactly.

"Who's that, honey?"

I exhaled. "Mon insisted on taking me to class."

My mother smiled.

"Don't get excited, Ma. It's just a ride."

"For now. I think he may be wearing you down!"

I kissed my mother on the cheek and grabbed my backpack. "I love you."

"I love you more, baby."

Chapter 5

Lemonte

"Why the fuck am I nervous? It's just Nia."
Thick, beautiful TaNia Monae.

I knocked on the door a second time before I
heard her voice say, "Hold on."

Grown-ass man, nervous about being around
a woman. A nigga was dumb paranoid. When I
thought of the perfect lady, the first person who
popped in my head had always been Nia. She
was literally everything I wanted in a woman.
Every time I made an attempt to make her mine,
she shut me down. Every single time, man. She
would say shit like I wasn't her type, she didn't
do hood niggas, I was too rough around the
edges. Usually, I didn't sweat shit like that, but
TaNia had this hook in me that I couldn't get out,
though I tried hard as hell. I wasn't the type of
dude to chase any female. Period. But I couldn't
shake Nia. So here I was all the way across town,

knocking on her mom's door. I knew I probably looked weak as fuck, but I couldn't help it.

I heard the locks turn, and I turned around at the same time she opened the door. Man, she was so beautiful.

"Damn, Mon," she whispered. "You gon' bang my door down?"

"You gon' keep me waiting?" I asked, smiling. I knew I was showing all thirty-two. I had two slugs at the bottom that covered my fang teeth, but those shits were showing too. It was crazy, because I never smiled, but she made me do shit out of the ordinary.

"I asked you to hold on," she said with attitude.

I never knew what I did to rub her the wrong way, but shit, I didn't care. Her bark was worse than her bite. "Yeah, but we also on a schedule, nerd."

She shook her head, slightly annoyed. "Whatever."

I took a moment to admire her. She was dressed down, which was different for her. Every time I saw her, she had on heels, but today she rocked Jordans and jeans, with her braids in a high bun on her head. She was just as sexy, though, just laidback. "You look good, ma."

"Thank you," she said, grabbing the strap of her backpack.

"I'll carry that for you."

She looked at me for a while before she handed the backpack over.

"This me right here," I said, pointing at my all-white 2015 Chevy Camaro.

She closed her door and locked it before she proceeded down the steps behind me. "I don't remember you having this. You, Key, and Marco must be doing well in the stripping business."

I knew that would be my main hurdle with her. She wasn't feeling the fact that I owned a strip club with my best friends. I mean, I could understand that, but a nigga had to eat someway somehow. I was trying to slowly transition from selling drugs to being a real businessman. I was only twenty-six, and already I was on the verge of being a millionaire. I didn't want to be in the drug game all my life like the OGs. I wanted to stack my bread up and actually live long enough to enjoy it. You couldn't let niggas know what type of moves you were making. So I invested. I franchised multiple restaurants, as well as owning one. I was also part owner of a strip club and pretty soon a hotel. I still had runners on the drug end, but I was done getting my hands dirty with that shit. I kept it low-key. I had a $30,000 car and two condos, one downtown not far from Key's loft and another one in Miami. I lived liked an ordinary-ass nigga making millionaire-ass money. My plan was to leave Dallas as soon as I got my ducks in a row.

I reached out and opened the car door for her so that she could get in. "Not gon' answer, huh?"

She got into the passenger seat, and I walked around the back of the car. She was putting her seat belt on when I sat in the driver seat. I tried not to look at her breasts as she bent down, but she had them sitting up, looking right. I owned a strip club. I saw breasts too much for my liking, but I wanted to help TaNia's escape her bra.

"No, I'm not."

I wasn't trying to beef with her right now. All I wanted to do was spend some time. "Where you wanna eat?"

She glanced in her side mirror, checking the bun of braids on top of her head. "Since you're basically kidnapping me, it doesn't matter."

What the hell, man? Never in my life had I experienced a woman like her. She didn't want to have shit to do with me. The money, the cars, the clothes didn't mean shit to her. She wasn't easily moved by the monetary support I could offer, more so because she had her own shit as well as the trust fund her pops left when he passed. But I was used to women throwing themselves at me. I really didn't know how to handle Nia. I wasn't trying to sound cocky, but I was an attractive man. If the eyes didn't get them, then surely the tats did. If all else failed, the dreads sealed the deal, but she wasn't impressed by any of that.

I thought about all the places I could take her and have her back in time for school. The last thing I wanted to do was make her late for class. She was serious about that shit, so I wouldn't get in the way. I'd always admired how focused she was about school, so I didn't want to do anything that would put myself in a bad position. "I got a little spot. You like seafood?"

"I love seafood."

I smiled. "One."

Nia glanced over at me. "One what?"

"One thing we have in common." I pulled the Camaro off the curb. Nia and her mom lived on the north side, in a suburb area where white folk stayed. She wasn't far from where I stayed downtown.

"So you're counting the things that make us compatible?"

"I am. I'm trying to make sure you know we are compatible."

Nia looked at me and laughed. "You're silly."

"Nah, I'm for real. I want us to get to know each other."

She nodded. "I can see that, if this kidnapping is anything to go by."

"Say, man. Stop saying that shit. I did not kidnap you."

She laughed and grabbed her phone from her clutch. She looked at me sideways for a moment. "Do you still sing?"

I laughed. "That's random as hell, but yeah, I still sing real low to myself."

"Will you sing for me?"

"You gon' twerk that ass if I do?"

She rolled her eyes and leaned back in her seat. "I can't with you, Lemonte," she said, laughing.

I turned up that "Wet Dreamz" by J. Cole, and we rode listening to that song on repeat. I stole glances at Nia as she looked out her window. I wondered what she was thinking. I didn't want to seem too thirsty but, man, I was feeling shorty. I knew she probably thought I was trying to take advantage of her, but that wasn't the case. I just wanted to be with her. Period.

When we arrived at the restaurant, I was sure to be the perfect gentleman. I opened her car door, held her hand as she got out, and held the restaurant door open. I followed her thick ass as she walked in. I picked a booth in the back because I didn't want us to be interrupted.

"So," I started once we were settled, "this your last year in school. I know you ready for that to be over." Not only was she sexy, but she was smart and determined. She didn't allow the things that she ran into in life deter her from her goals. I thought that fact about her made her even more beautiful.

"I am sooo glad I'm almost done," she said, smiling as she looked over the menu. "I feel like I been in school forever." She looked up at me and smiled. "I remember a certain somebody telling me that they were looking into classes. Did that ever happen?" She looked at me sideways.

I shook my head. "No, ma'am. I've been extremely busy, Nia. I don't—"

"Have time," she said, finishing my statement. "You don't have time for much, Mon, but you always seem to make time."

"I know that," I said, looking at her. "I'm going to look into it. I need a degree up under my belt." I smiled. "But what you want to eat, though?"

She'd put the menu down and had her phone in her hand, probably texting Tori. "It doesn't matter. Just make sure you get me the salad as well."

At that moment, our waiter walked up. V was fresh out of high school on his way to college. He approached me on some "let me run for you" bullshit, but I shot that down. I didn't want him risking his freedom and future for me, so I offered him work here at the restaurant making fifteen dollars an hour, keeping all the tips he made. It wasn't dope boy money, but it was enough for him.

I looked over at V, who was still looking at Nia. I knew his dilemma. He probably wanted to take his eyes off her and couldn't. "Pick ya jaw up, V."

He finally looked over at me and laughed. "Sorry, boss."

"Boss," TaNia said, smiling at him and making him blush hard. "Let's not make his head any bigger than it already is, V."

V nodded as he looked at me. "What would you like to order?"

"Two of the seafood salads overloaded with shrimp, both grilled and fried. Bring us two sweet teas as well."

V nodded. "Coming right out."

"I need it immediately. I have somewhere else to be, and don't forget, I pay you."

He laughed as he walked away.

I sat there for a minute in my thoughts as Nia continued to scroll through her phone. I wondered if she knew how I felt about her, how I always felt. I felt like it was now or never. I needed her to know.

She scrunched up her face and twisted her mouth as she looked at me. She was so fucking cute. "What did you mean, you pay him?"

I smiled at her. "This is one of my spots."

Her eyes got big as she looked at me sideways. "As in you own this restaurant?"

"As in I own this restaurant. I franchise a few others as well."

She looked at me, confused and trying to process what I just said. "Wait, what?"

"I have a few restaurants that I invested in with Marco and Key. We ain't trying to just own a strip club, which was just the beginning. Mrs. Gordon came to me last year, telling me about the financial situation that she was in. She was on the verge of losing this place. I couldn't let that happen. I remember when we were in school, when Key and Tori first started talking, we used to all come here and eat." I laughed at the memory. "I was trying to get at you even way back then, and you were curving me. Made me feel like I was an ugly dude or something. Anyway, Mrs. Gordon wanted me to buy it, so I did."

Nia looked at me smiling.

"What's up?" I asked.

"I had no idea, Lemonte," she said, never removing her smile. "And you saved this place for her?

Let me find out you have a heart underneath all this hard hood dude stuff you got going on."

"I'm trying to be a good man."

"I see you making progress. I'm proud of you, Lemonte."

I fought this smile with all I had, and this motherfucker still appeared. "You proud of me?"

"I am," she said, smiling. "I remember when you were nickel and diming, and now you on your grown man. I can't do nothing but respect that."

"I'm too old to still be in the game. I'm wrapping up some things to be completely done with it."

TaNia looked at me and smiled. "You are old, though. Ain't you like thirty?"

"Real funny."

Nia laughed as she returned to looking at her phone. I reached over and took her phone out of her hand. "You gon' just be rude like that?"

Nia looked at her phone in my hands. "Can I have my phone, please?"

"No. We together. You have to be in class in forty-five minutes. I want you to talk to me."

V came back with our salads and set them in front of us. "Enjoy," he said before he walked off.

"About?" She grabbed her salad and put ranch dressing all over it.

I looked at her. "Us."

She stopped pouring her ranch to look at me. "What about us?"

I grabbed my fork and mixed my salad. I'd played this conversation over and over in my head. I knew all the things I wanted to say to convince her that giving me a shot was the right choice. But all that prepping I did flew out the fucking window.

"I just . . . Shit, I don't know, Nia."

She looked at me like I was crazy. I knew my demeanor was throwing her off. I was by nature a chill dude. I didn't feel a need to yell or be all in a person's face to get my point across. But now my palms were sweaty, and I was stumbling over my words. Shit was crazy.

"What you mean you don't know, Mon?" Nia was leaned back in her seat, looking at me. I threw my arm over her shoulder and pulled her closer to me. She smelled so fucking good. She was so soft against me. "I want to do whatever you want to do." *What the fuck does that even mean?*

She smiled. "What does that mean?"

I ran my hand down my face and laughed. I was about to make my move on Nia. I looked over at her, and she had her bottom lip tucked into her mouth, suppressing her laugh.

"You eating this up, huh?"

She shook her head. "I don't know what you talking about."

"Yes, you do, ma."

Nia shook her head as she continued to eat her salad.

I sat back in my chair, stressed the fuck out, as she continued to eat her salad like she didn't have a care in the world.

I removed my arm from the back of the chair and started eating my salad as well. I felt like a nerd asking the baddest chick in the world out. I just knew Nia was out of my league. Trying to get her was a fucking reach on my end, but it was a risk I was willing to take.

"I know I asked this earlier, but why me, Lemonte? I mean, you can have any girl."

"Apparently, I can't have any girl," I said, looking at her.

"You know what I mean."

I didn't understand why she kept asking why her as if picking her was a bad thing. "I mean, Nia—"

"All these years I never got it! You keep asking me out, and I keep telling you no in hopes that you would just let up on whatever mission you are on. I'm not the type of girl dudes like you go after. I'm okay with that!"

I didn't understand what she meant. I knew it wasn't an insecurity thing, because she had dudes coming at her left and right. She knew she was beautiful. Everyone with eyes knew that.

"Dudes like me? TaNia, that's offensive."

"I'm not trying to offend you," she rushed to say. "It's not like that, Lemonte. I consider you a friend."

"I ain't trying to be your friend."

She looked at me for the longest time before she returned to eating her salad. I took that as a clue that she didn't want to continue having this conversation. This was turning into a bad situation quick. I didn't know what the problem was. "I know I'm hood. I can't change that. The dreads and the tats and shit. But I'm a good dude, Nia. I know you out . . ."

I stopped talking when I noticed she had her head down and was playing with her food. I didn't know if the change in the atmosphere was because of something I said or a mistake I made, but I didn't want to piss Nia off.

"Look, Nia. I don't want anyone else but you. It's been like that for years, and I don't see that changing anytime soon. I want you! Why? I just do, all right? I don't know why the hell I do outside of the reasons I already expressed. You are just different. I love everything about you."

She looked at me as if she knew I was running game, but I wasn't. I was being as real as I could with her.

"You love everything about me?"

I leaned in closer to her face, so she could hear me. "I love every single thing about you. I don't see what's not to like. If you give me a chance to show you how much I'm feeling you, then you wouldn't have an ounce of doubt about it in that pretty little head of yours."

I knew getting her to come around would be a task, but I wasn't giving up. I had to have her. She had my undivided attention, and no matter how much I attempted to stay away from her, I was always drawn right back. I was always right back sniffing behind her. It was just her. TaNia didn't want to accept it, but she belonged to me.

Chapter 6

Keyton

"I need to get off the phone, Key!"

I smirked as I continued to count the drawer from the bar. I wasn't trying to hear that "get off the phone" shit Tori was spitting! "What time you gon' make it home?" Like I didn't know that already.

"I have the same schedule I've been having all month," she sassed.

"Say, cut out the attitude. I'll see you when you get home, crybaby. I love you," I said as I hung up the phone.

I finished the count and placed bands around the fifty stacks in front of me. I was so ready to get home and lie under my wife I couldn't see straight. I looked up when a knock sounded on my door. It was a coded knock only my team knew. I had a small circle of men I trusted, and I wasn't quick to accept just anybody. I went by the motto, "You are who you eat with." I wouldn't allow fakes in my circle. I couldn't afford shit like that.

"Come in," I said.

Marco walked in with a bag in his hand, and I already knew what it was. When it came to loyalty, Lemonte, Cortez, and Marco were on point. Those were my brothers, though we were birthed from different mothers. There wasn't much they couldn't get out of me, and I knew the same stood for them.

Marco was way more than my driver. He was ex-military and could kill a man with his bare hands if need be. I met him while I was still in high school. I was peddling drugs for a big-time dope dealer, Flacco. Flacco was killed for crossing his connect, who turned out to be part of the Cartel. Everybody knew not to fuck with the Cartel. Marco was sent to kill everyone who was affiliated with Flacco.

From the runners up to his head niggas in charge, Mon and I were on that list. On some real shit, I requested a meeting with the man who ordered the hit on a suicide mission. I wanted to clear my name and let them know that Mon and I weren't with that bullshit. After much convincing, they allowed me and Mon to walk away with our lives and in turn created a bond between Marco and me that would never be broken. I trusted him with my life, even though at one point he was the man assigned to take it.

"Wassup, boss," I said as I stood and greeted Marco. We weren't only brothers. We were business partners. We split all the profit from the club as well as the restaurants. I ran the club while Mon held down the restaurants. We were working on the finishing touches on the hotel that Marco would have the most control of. His loyalty to me was enough for me to respect him, but the fact that he was willing to go to war for me and mines made me respect him more. He was twenty-eight and had been through hell on earth, but he was loyal to the people he cared about. He didn't speak until he had something to say, and he didn't have much to say often. His skill set was that of a sniper, but he had a background that involved boxing and martial arts as well. Every squad needed a Marco.

"I got the drop," he said as he set the bag on the table. "I'm so fucking glad that's almost the last drop I'll ever make."

"I know, bro. I'm so over all this hustling shit." I looked him over and could tell something was a little off with him. "What's up, Marco? You got something on your mind?"

He exhaled as he looked around. "We got a new girl," he said, smiling.

I smiled back. "Yeah, nigga, we got a few. Which one you talking about?"

He smirked. "The chocolate, thick one. The finest fucking one, bro. I need to have that."

"You talking about Winter."

He frowned. "That's not what they call her."

"Storm is her stage name."

"Yeah, man, fucking Storm. She has gray eyes, my nigga. I tried talking to her, but she ain't have shit for me. She straight curved my ass. I'm gon' get her, though. Say, what you know about her?"

In all the years I'd known Marco, he'd never shown interest in a female. I mean, he knocked them down all the fucking time, but he never spoke of one in this aspect. Winter had this fool wide open. I couldn't front and say she wasn't bad, because shorty was banging. She looked like the model Miracle Watts, only with gray eyes. She was a beautiful woman. And though she was a stripper, unlike most of the broads here, this wasn't shorty's last stop. She was just passing through.

"She goes to UNT with Tori and Nia."

Marco frowned. "She in school? She has to be mad young then."

I nodded. "She twenty-five. She in her last year like Nia and Tori. Believe it or not, she's going into business management. They'll all graduate together. She learned about the position through Tori. But, uh, I don't know much else."

"She is fucking gorgeous. I want her."

I smiled as I leaned up in my chair. "You've never had an issue getting ladies, Marco. Fuck is up now?"

"She treats me like an ugly nigga, bro. She be curving my ass left to right," he said, laughing. "Say, call her sexy ass up here and tell her to stop treating her coworkers wrong."

"That shit petty as fuck," I said, laughing my ass off.

"Nigga, do you want me to file a formal complaint?"

"Hell no," I said, grabbing my phone and shooting Cortez a text to bring Storm to my office. "I ain't doing all that fucking paperwork."

About ten minutes passed before Winter knocked on the office door.

I saw the smile that crept across Marco's face as he stood in the corner of my office. "She gon' murder my ass."

"Come in," I said, looking at the door.

Winter walked in with a confused look on her face. She was dressed in a pink jumpsuit with her hair flowing past her shoulders. She didn't have an ounce of makeup on, and she was still gorgeous. I understood Marco's dilemma.

"Yes, boss?"

"Come in, Winter. Have a seat," I said, standing to allow her to sit.

She looked over at Marco and frowned.

"Hello, Winter," he said, smiling at her.

She nodded and sat down. "Does he have to be here?" she asked, gesturing toward Marco.

Marco laughed. "What did I ever do to you?"

Winter looked back at him. "Nothing, it's just that if this is an issue with me, then I don't get why you're here."

"You know I'm your boss, right?"

Winter nodded. "I'm well aware. Does it take two of you for this discussion, though?"

Marco laughed and shook his head. "I'm here because I can be. Is that a good enough answer?"

She rolled her eyes and turned back to me. "Whatever."

I shook my head. Lately, my niggas had been getting me into all types of shit. "Umm, Winter, I had a complaint submitted to me with regard to your behavior toward your coworkers."

"Coworkers or boss?" she said, looking back at Marco.

"Your behavior is the issue, Winter," Marco said, smiling.

She turned to look at Marco. "I'm assuming you submitted the complaint."

"I did. I don't like the way you treat me," Marco said, walking over to her.

She stood and got in his face. "What, because I'm not like all these other bitches throwing their panties at you?"

Marco licked his lips as he looked down at her. "I ain't say throw your panties, but damn, you don't have to be rude."

"I'm not rude. I just don't tolerate bullshit."

Marco looked offended. "So, I'm bullshit?"

"I didn't say that, Marco. I'm just saying that I don't tolerate it. If I was rude to you I apologize, but I see all these girls in your face trying to fuck you, and it's just not that kind of party this way."

Marco moved closer to her as if I weren't in the room and they weren't in my office. That's the thing about Marco, he didn't take no for an answer, and he wasn't stopping until he got what he wanted. He had Winter in his scope. "I didn't say that's what I wanted. I'm just trying to be your friend—"

"I got enough of those," she said, interrupting him.

He exhaled deeply as he squinted his eyes at her. I couldn't contain my laugh.

He turned to me, frowning. "You think this shit funny? She is mean as shit for no reason," he said, looking back at Winter.

"You can get over it, though, right?" she asked, placing her hands on her hips.

"Nah, I can't," Marco said, stepping closer to her. "You gon' be nice, right?"

She smiled at him for the first time, and he smiled back. "You gon' make me?"

"Hell yeah," he said close to her face. "I will if I have to. Baby girl, I can fix all that shit."

Winter looked him over for a moment before she turned to me. "Are we done here?"

I smiled. "Yes, sweetheart."

"Watch your attitude, Winter," Marco warned again as she marched off.

She smiled at me then turned to flip him off. She was gon' give his ass a run for his money, but by the look on Marco's face, he wasn't letting shit die down.

Chapter 7

Demarco

I had to watch that ass as she walked out. I didn't know why the fuck a woman as beautiful as she was chose to be a stripper, but this lifestyle wasn't for little momma at all. I didn't know what the fuck it was about her, but I wanted her ass something serious. I didn't trip off of women. I didn't have time for that. I could knock down any female I wanted and keep it moving, but something about Winter was completely different, and I wanted to do things differently. I knew she couldn't stand my ass, but I had other plans for her. I wanted her. Simply put, I got what I wanted.

"She gon' kick yo' ass, Marco," Key said, laughing.

I joined in with him as I headed toward the door. "I don't know why she don't like my ass, man. I need to show her the real me. I'm a gentle giant."

Key looked at me for a moment before he burst out laughing. I laughed too and shook my head, because on the outside looking in that shit was far from the truth. I never learned how to love anyone. I knew that sounded crazy coming from a grown man, but it was true.

From a very young age, I'd been on my own. I was born Demarco Donte Montgomery, but I didn't know who named me or if my name meant anything to anyone. I lived on the streets, under bridges, and in homeless shelters. From as far back as I could remember, I'd been a ward of the state, but the state ain't never gave me shit. I didn't know who my parents were, and at this point, I didn't care. I just remember adopting a mentality to eat or get ate. Before I went to the Marines, I didn't have shit. It took so much for me to get accepted because I physically wasn't in a position to go. I had to gain weight and adopt some type of training skills. I would go to the free boxing classes hosted at the recreation center during the day and back to the shelters and bridges at night. During the boxing lesson, the recreation center tacked on mixed martial arts as well as Tae Kwon Do, so I joined those classes as well.

The more I stayed at the recreation center, the less I had to sleep under the bridge or at one of them bum-ass shelters. I did everything in my power to get into the military. As soon as I turned eighteen, I enlisted. I stayed in for about six years until I met Lou, one of the heads of the Cartel. Shortly after I made it up to sergeant, I met Lou off base at a shooting range. I had a particular skill set that he needed. I was a top-ranked sniper for the Marines, and I had definitely built up muscle and physique during my time there. He needed a hit man, a killer, and a fighter. He needed me. I wanted to remain in the Marines, but the numbers he threw at me made my leaving worth it. I was killing innocent people then. At least the motherfuckers I took out now deserved to die or were at my head. I felt a certain level of loyalty to the Cartel, but when I found an escape where I did little to no killing at all, I jumped on it.

Working with Key and Mon was what I needed. Those were my brothers, and no matter what, I had their backs because I knew they had mines. The dynamic of our friendship was weird being that I was initially sent to kill them, but when I saw that they came to the heads of the Cartel and let them know that they weren't a part of the shit Flacco had going, I knew that they were different dudes. Lou hated to see me go, but he understood. I was tired of having nightmares and shit.

I wanted to live a life as normal as possible, and I saw myself breaking out of the hard, "fuck feelings" demeanor I adopted. I needed a change, a breath of fresh air. I just knew that was Winter.

"She about to perform right now," Key said, looking down at the calendar.

I smiled because I knew he was aware of what I was thinking. Her ass wasn't getting away that easily. "Bet. I'm gon' holla at you about that other shit tomorrow. Once I talk to shawty, I'ma be out."

Key stood up to dap me up, and I quickly embraced him. "Be safe, bro."

"Always, Key. I'll hit you later," I said as I walked out the door.

I made it down to the stage in record time to watch as she walked out to sit in a chair in the middle of the stage. She wore this all-black lace number that showcased all of her curves. Her jet-black hair, which was in big curls, fell past her shoulders as she grabbed the back of the chair and straddled it backward. I made sure I stood in direct view of her so that she could see that I was in attendance, like always. She looked at me and smirked before she bent backward over the chair as her song started. She had the attention of every person in the room as Jeremiah's "Fuck You All the Time" dropped.

Even Tonya, the bartender, had stopped serving drinks.

She stood straight up and made her ass bounce. Bills flew everywhere as she grabbed the pole and climbed it halfway. Spreading her legs wide, she twerked her ass while holding on, going around the pole in a slow motion while now Lil Wayne rapped in the background. I wanted to snatch her ass down, but I was enjoying the show too much. She turned to me and walked slowly toward me. I had to take a deep breath to control myself. She mouthed the next words to me directly while she crawled on the stage as close to me as she could get: *I hit you like what you sayin'. I could fuck you all the time. I could fuck you all the time.*

When the song ended, she smiled at me before she stood to walk off the stage. Everyone was on their feet, clapping for her. I went straight to the back exit where I knew she would be leaving, and I waited by the door. I pulled out my blunt and rested my Timbs against the wall as I watched the ladies walk out one by one. I had to admit we had some bad dancers, but not one I'd seen held a candle to Winter. This woman was fucking beautiful. From her gray eyes to her long, jet-black hair and her thick-ass, cornbread-fed body, she had a nigga wide open, and I had to have her.

"Hey, Marco," one of the strippers said, running her hands along my jacket. I hit her ass with a nod as I blew smoke out. I wasn't trying to have another chick in my face when Winter walked out. She kept it moving, and I definitely appreciated that. Winter was the last one to exit, and she looked tired. When she spotted me, she crunched up her sexy-ass face and rolled her eyes.

"This has to be harassment, though, Marco," she said, expressing herself with her hands as she threw her bag over her shoulder.

I laughed as I grabbed the bag to carry it for her. "I ain't harassing you. Why you so mean, Winter? Damn, you act like you can't even have a conversation with me. You can't tease me like that and expect a man to just let you walk away."

"I was performing."

"Bullshit," I said, laughing. "You had me ready to jump on stage wit'cho ass."

She smirked at me then nodded. "So what's up?"

"I need to talk to you."

She rolled her eyes again as she pushed the back door open while I followed her. "Let me guess," she said once we got outside. "You want to save me?"

"What the fuck?" I said, frowning. "I don't know a lot of shit, Winter. But I know you don't need anyone to save you." I smiled as I looked dead into her eyes. "If anything, ma, I need you to save me."

She turned to me and crossed her arms over her chest. "Save you from what?"

She may have thought I was joking, but I wasn't. I needed somebody to take my mind off the past. I needed to get over this shit. I adjusted her bag on my shoulder. "Myself."

I expected her to laugh, but she didn't. She looked at me harder and let silence fall between us. It was weird because I almost felt intimidated by her. As if she could see a part of me that I wasn't yet ready to expose.

"Why do I need to save you from yourself, Demarco?"

I smiled for the umpteenth time. I was tripping off that because I never smile for shit. "You gon' hit me with the real name?"

"Isn't that your real name?"

"It is," I admitted, looking at her.

"What's your entire name?"

I looked at her sideways. "What, you the Feds or some shit?"

She shook her head and laughed, causing her dimple in her cheek to deepen. "Hell no! I hate cops! Especially bad ones. They kill people for no reason and get put on administrative leave. The shit irks me."

"I feel you on that," I said, attempting to swerve her question.

"I'll give you mines first, since I see that you're uncomfortable. It's Winter Sky Malone."

"That's sexy as fuck. It fits you well."

She laughed again. "What the hell is sexy about Winter Sky Malone?"

"I don't know, maybe because you saying it in that sexy-ass voice. Yeah," I said, licking my lips. "That's it."

She blushed as she looked at me.

"It's Demarco Donte Montgomery."

She smiled at me and bit into her thick-ass bottom lip. She had me ready to pounce on her little ass.

"Now, that's sexy."

"That shit wack as hell," I said, laughing hard.

She laughed with me for a moment before she looked up at me. "I think I may like you, Demarco.

I licked my lips and smiled. "I'm on that same shit, Winter."

She exhaled deeply. "I see a million girls in your face all night, Demarco. I avoid situations like that."

I knew that was the issue. Every time she saw a chick in my face, she would roll her eyes and shake her head at me, but that shit wasn't what it looked like. They were my workers. Point blank period. "They work for me, Winter."

"Yes, I understand that, but it's so constant that it's annoying. Then you try to talk to me, and I don't want to be looked at as one of those chicks fucking my way to the top. I'm just here to make money and go! I don't need any extra drama."

"I wouldn't put you in that position, ma. I don't usually fraternize with dancers, but you make me forget that rule. You throw me off, and I find myself watching you when I'm supposed to be watching the room. I just want a chance to know the woman who has me so captivated."

She laughed at me, basically calling bullshit, and I just shook my head. Her ass had me out here sounding corny as fuck, but shit, it didn't matter. It was Winter.

"I'll go to lunch with you," she finally said, going into her purse and pulling out her phone as we began walking to her car.

I couldn't stop the smile that spread across my face. "Bet. That's all I need."

She continued to look at me. "You promise to be a perfect gentleman? Because that's all I date."

I licked my lips and nodded. "I promise."

She turned to me and smiled when we made it to her 2015 Camry. "I'm giving you a chance, Marco. Please don't take me lightly when I say that I don't tolerate bullshit."

"I don't tolerate bullshit either, so we gon' get along!"

She smirked at me as I grabbed her phone and programmed my number into her it. She burst out laughing when she saw how I saved it. "Marco Daddy Number Two? Really?"

I smiled as she opened her car door, and I placed her bag in the back seat. "Hell yeah," I said as I leaned into her driver window. "You don't have to worry about me and bullshit, Winter. I don't fuck with these girls on that level. Not one of them can say they did anything with me. No head, no fuckin', no nothing. I'm a businessman, and I handle my shit as such. But you, Winter Malone, make me forget all that shit."

She tried to hide her blush but I saw it, and it just made me smile harder.

"Text me," she said as she cranked her car. "Tonight."

"Yes, ma'am," I said as she pulled off.

Chapter 8

Winter

I knew accepting Marco's date was going to come back and bite me in my ass, but I couldn't keep dodging him, and if I was honest with myself, I wanted to know more about him. He was so mysterious, always quiet, never smiling. He pulled me in with a look or head gesture. I mean, this man stayed on my mind constantly. I knew it had a lot to do with how attractive he was.

His body was perfection with clothes on, so I could just imagine how he looked with his clothes off. He was about six feet nine inches with a muscular build that made me wanna climb him. The smooth light-toned skin he had was covered in tattoos. He had these dark, mysterious eyes that I got lost in every time I looked at him. He had thick, full lips he loved to lick, and his beard covered half of his perfect oval face. I mean, he personified sexiness and held lust at his fingertips, and to hell with me because I was on his fucking hook. I always saw him watching me, but I wondered if he knew I was a fan of his as well. I meant what I said to him. I respected his position, and I didn't want him to think of me as one of those females who didn't care about their reputation. You know, those women who fuck everybody they need to to get to the top. I never understood those types. I was determined to get mines on my own, and that wasn't a trait about me that would ever change.

Anyway, I was happy as hell to be off. I couldn't wait for this semester to be over, because school was grinding on my last nerve. I was almost finished getting my master's degree in accounting with a minor in business management. My five-year plan was to have my accounting firm open by the time I turned thirty. I had five years to get my shit together, and working at Pure was the only way to come up with my tuition and build my savings up for when I made my move.

As soon as I got into my apartment, my clothes came off. I always felt so gross when I came in from work. I couldn't lie on my bed or sit on my furniture until I washed my ass. I was naturally lazy, believe it or not, with all the stuff I had going on. Don't get me wrong, I kept my hygiene up and my apartment was always spotless, but outside of that, I didn't do shit. I worked at a club, so I didn't feel the need to do that. I didn't have time to kick it or do no other shit because I was focused on graduation. My parents always said I was going to grow old and lonely with a whole bunch of cats. I could see that happening.

After staying in the shower for about thirty minutes, I was finally wrinkled enough to get out. Momma said, "If it doesn't squeak, it ain't clean." The more I thought about it, the more I realized that my momma was hell.

After rubbing myself down with scented lotion and slipping on my teddy, I crawled in my king-sized bed and cuddled under my dark purple comforter as my body slid across my silk sheets.

"Yessssss," I moaned as I reached to grab my phone and the remote off the nightstand beside me. I flicked on the television as my phone buzzed, indicating a text. I smiled when I saw that *Love & Basketball* was playing. That was my shit. That smile immediately faded when I saw who texted me.

Ex Bullshit: Sup, ma?

Me: Shit.

Ex Bullshit: Damn, Winter. You always on ten, ma. You need some dick?

I shook my head and laughed at his dumb ass. He didn't see it as an issue that he was a lying, cheating, worthless piece of shit. Me needing dick was always the problem. I mean, I could use a good session, but that didn't have anything to do with how I felt about his extra dumb ass.

Ex Bullshit: 'Cause I gotcha, Storm.

I rolled my eyes as I threw my phone on the opposite end of the bed. I wasn't dealing with him right now. I had school in the morning, and I was trying to relax. I hated his guts. Bastard.

When my phone indicated I had another text, I wasn't going to answer it, but I decided to do so anyway. I blushed at the name on the screen.

Marco Daddy #2: What are you doing, beautiful?

Me: Lying in bed.

Marco Daddy #2: I'm jealous of that motherfucker then.

I laughed as I replied.

Me: It's very comfortable.

Marco Daddy #2: I'm comfortable too. You can lie on me.

I rolled my eyes and sucked my teeth before I responded.

Me: You don't do this often, do you?

Marco Daddy #2: What?

Me: Text

Marco Daddy #2: Not often, nah. But I'm willing to step out of my comfort zone to impress you. I must be pretty bad at this shit for you to say that. LMAO

Me: LOL! I've heard better.

Marco Daddy #2: Aww shit.

Me: I'll give you a pass this time.

Marco Daddy #2: I appreciate that. So when we going on this date?

Me: Whenever we both free.

Marco Daddy #2: You don't have another day off scheduled for about a month out. We gotta change that shit because I ain't waiting that long.

Me: I'm not worth the wait?

Marco Daddy #2: I have been waiting since I laid eyes on you. I don't think it's cool to keep me waiting. I'm the boss. I'll remove you from the schedule for the weekend. We can go tomorrow.

Me: Don't! I can't take off right now. Can we wait until next week sometime?

Marco Daddy #2: Damn, you really gon' make me wait that long?

Me: Sorry, but I need the money.

It took him a minute to respond, so I knew he was pissed, but I did need the money. I wasn't saying no just to say it.

Marco Daddy #2: Bet

I exhaled as I lay back down. I really wanted to kick it with him. Maybe I would reconsider letting him take me off the schedule. I remembered Quincy and Monica fucking, and then I was knocked out. I thought my brain was waiting for that scene before it shut down. I needed some companionship around this camp.

When I woke up the next morning and the sun was shining, I knew that I had overslept. "Damn," I mumbled as I climbed to the end of my bed to grab my phone. My alarm had gone off two hours ago. I closed my eyes and let my head fall back on my fluffy pillows as I exhaled. "Oh, well hell. I'm mu'fuckin' tired, anyway," I said, imitating Young Thug's daughter.

My phone rang in my hand, and I smiled as I answered it. "Good morning, Ma!"

"Good morning, Winter. I miss you! You're always at work or school! When are you coming to see us?"

I lived about thirty minutes away from my parents, but since I was working at the club, I kept my distance. My parents had no idea what I did for a living. They thought I went to the University of North Texas on an academic scholarship, which I did have, but it wasn't full, so I still had to foot the bill for my education. I definitely wouldn't allow my parents to pay, because like I said, I like making my own way.

"I'll come see you guys this weekend, Momma, I promise. I've been so busy! I barely get any sleep, but I miss you guys too, so I'll be there before you know it."

"I'm going to hold you to that, Sky!"

I smiled. My mother addressing me by my middle name was her term of endearment. "Where's Daddy?"

"He just stepped out. He misses you too, Sky. Your little brother hasn't laid eyes on you in months."

I slumped down on my bed, feeling bad. "I'm sorry, Ma. I promise to come around more. I love you all!"

"We love you more, Winter."

I talked to my mom for about twenty more minutes about everything from my dating life to school, food, my apartment, then back to my dating life. She wanted grandchildren, and being that my brother, Darien, was only thirteen, they were looking for me to give it to them. Not happening.

I lay in my bed for another hour before I made a move. I needed to shop. I needed groceries and hygiene items. I figured I might as well make the best of the day since I missed class. I didn't have to be back at work until nine tonight, so I decided to hit the mall up. It felt like I hadn't been to the mall in years.

***

Coming out of Bath & Body Works, I ran into Tori and Nia. I hadn't known them that long, but the vibe I got from them was always cool. They were real women who had their shit together. I couldn't knock that.

"Heyyyy, Winter," Tori said, walking up to me with a smiling Nia behind her.

"Hey, y'all," I exclaimed as I hugged them. "Why you heffas didn't tell me y'all was coming to the mall? Let me find out!"

"Girl, it wasn't like that," TaNia said. "Hell, we had to run from Key and Mon asses. They got some shit with them and got us on some leashes. We escaped."

We all laughed because I knew that was true. Everyone knew who Tori and Nia were because they belonged to the bosses.

"That's crazy." I shook my head. "So what y'all got planned for today? I don't have to work until nine and I been overloaded with work and school. I need to turn up!"

"What you trying to do?" Nia asked.

I shrugged. "I don't know. I just know I want to do something."

"Well, let us know because I'm always down for a quick turn up."

"We can figure out something. I ain't trying to get crazy, but maybe Dave & Buster's or Main Event."

"Cool," Tori said, nodding. I saw Tori and Nia both look behind me, and I just knew there was about to be some shit. I felt somebody walk up behind me, and I didn't think much of the shit until they grabbed my ass.

I turned around, and there was Reggie's dog ass. You know, "Ex Bullshit."

"What the fuck, Reggie?"

"You can't have that mutherfucka sitting in my face and expect me not to smack that shit," he said with a sexy smirk on his face. I wished his ass was ugly, but he was far from it. He was about six feet three inches, with smooth caramel skin and a full beard, an incredible body, and thick, sexy lips that I looked at every time they moved. If only he weren't a dog, I thought we could have worked, but I couldn't do that "stressing behind a dude" crap. I was too fly for all that.

"You touch me again and I'll embarrass you! That ain't yours to touch, playboy!"

"That's gon' forever belong to me. Quit playin'," he said, looking around me. "Hey, ladies," he said to Nia and Tori. They smiled and spoke back. He looked back at me. "When we gon' kick it?"

"No time soon, playboy," I said as I turned back around. "I'm busy, and I don't have time for the bull."

"I'm bullshit?" he said, sounding pissed off.

I knew he was about to show his ass, so I just braced myself.

"So, you shake your ass for dollars, but that ain't bullshit?" he said, getting in my face. I crossed my arms over my chest as I looked down at the ground. "Don't hold your head down now. You do that shit every night like you proud of it."

"Get the fuck out my face," I said, pushing him. He didn't budge, and that just pissed me off more.

"You mad? You don't like to hear about yourself, huh? Mommy and Daddy know their precious little Winter is really a stripper bitch named Storm?"

"What the hell?" TaNia said, stepping between us. "Uh, fool, it's time for you to go."

He looked TaNia up and down, licking his lips before he shook his head and stepped back. "I'ma holla at you later, Storm."

"I can't stand his ass," I said, trying to control my emotions. I was shocked at TaNia. She hardly ever said shit, but she took up for me. "Thanks, TaNia," I mumbled.

TaNia waved her hand dismissively. "He cute and all, but he wack as hell."

"I was back here plotting on how we could take his big ass down," Tori said, laughing.

"I promise he stays popping up on me. I think he stalking me low-key."

"Well, we ain't gon' trip on him. Let's go!"

I decided to take Tori's advice and not trip. I needed to get loose, and I wasn't going to let Reggie stop me.

"Let's do this," Nia said. "How about you call in and we go to the damn club anyway? I'm sure Key and Mon won't trip."

I didn't really want to miss my money, but I did need a break. I was with it. "Cool."

"Aye," Tori said, slightly twerking as we walked off laughing.

Chapter 9

Lemonte

I saw her the moment she walked in. I believed everyone saw her. It'd been about two weeks since our date, and so far, she wasn't budging on that friend shit. I wasn't trying to be friends with her sexy ass, though, and she knew that. Damn, I was so glad she decided to come. I took a swig of my Cîroc Pineapple and watched her as she walked hand in hand with Tori and Winter to the bar. She looked good enough to eat. I would do just that if the chance was given. She wore her braids down, falling almost to her thick ass. She and Tori both wore all white, while Winter rocked all black. They were killing shit. Nia was dressed to impress like always. She wore a white bandage dress that stopped right above her knee and black pumps with white-and-black accessories. Every curve she had was on full display.

"That ain't cool," I said out loud. I had to give Tori and Winter their props also. They looked good too. I knew Key would be on her ass in minutes, and Marco would surely have Winter's ass for that catsuit she had on. But Nia took the cake for me. She had this glow about her as she walked. She leaned with her side to the bar as her eyes roamed around the building. She couldn't just come to my club and shut shit down. It wasn't long before some bum dude was in her face. That made my blood boil. "Who the fuck is this nigga?" I said out loud again as if someone could hear me. I immediately grabbed my cell phone from my pocket and dialed the head of security, Cortez.

He answered after one ring. "Yeah, boss?"

I exhaled. "Shorty at the bar with the white dress on."

"Yeah, boss. I saw her fine thick ass when she walked in."

This motherfucker! "Stop looking, nigga. That's all me! That clown in her face, kick his ass out!" I sipped my drink. I was already stressed the fuck out, and she just got here.

"Any motherfucker in her face gets put the fuck out! Refund their ass, and walk them out the door. Same procedure you take with Tori, Cortez." I hung up on his ass. I never took my eyes off her. She was in my spot and had the nerve to have this fuck nigga in her face. Not only that, she was laughing and entertaining dude like that shit would fly with me.

I heard the elevator behind me, and I knew it was Key. Me, him, and Marco were the only ones with the code. He came up to stand beside me, looking down through the glass. He stood there just looking for a moment before he spotted Tori.

"Fuck is she doing here?" It was clear he was pissed off. "Who is that nigga in Nia face? What the fuck is Winter doing? She curved Marco and called in. I thought she had an emergency. That dude is gon' flip out! He's not use to the chase and he definitely ain't gon' rock with being dissed just to run into her here. They bold as hell, huh?"

I shifted in my stance, the nine on my hip getting heavier by the minute, itching to be put into action. "I don't fucking know, but if Cortez doesn't get to his ass soon, I'm gon' have to handle shit on my own."

I pulled my phone out again and called Nia. I watched as she stopped her conversation with ol' boy to reach into her clutch for her phone then answer. The music around her drowned out her voice, but I still heard her when she spoke. "Yes?"

"Say, you know that nigga, ma?"

She looked up at the one-way glass and knew she had been spotted. Covering one ear with her finger, she pressed the phone closer to her ear so she could hear. "Does it matter?"

"To me it does," I said, getting more pissed by the minute. "Tell his ass to move around, Nia. Now! I'm not playing wit'cho ass, either."

"Who the fuck made you my daddy?"

I heard Tori say, "Ohhh shit!" in the background.

I slammed my drink down on the table. I was all out of character at this point. Yelling was just not me. "The fuck you mean? I'm saying, ma. Tell that nigga to bounce, or I'll take care of that shit for you."

I heard her suck her teeth. "Bye, Mon." I watched as she placed her phone back into her purse.

I looked at my phone for a minute before I had to laugh. "Yo, she hung up on my ass."

Key shook his head, laughing. "Between her and Tori, man, I don't know who worse," he laughed. "You better than me, though, 'cause that nigga would be knocked the fuck out," he said.

"Yo, that nigga 'bout to get stomped the fuck out!" I went to walk past Key when he grabbed me.

"Whoa, whoa, hold up, bruh! Cortez is handling it! Look," he said, pointing down to where Cortez was escorting the dude out. "He took care of it."

I grabbed my drink off the table and finished off what I didn't spill. "I wish I could just find another woman, man. This thing with Nia is too fucking much. I've been chasing her too long. I haven't hit any other bitches in weeks, man. I'm stressed out! All this pussy I'm missing chasing her ass. I could have any bitch, man, but no! I'm fucking stuck on stupid on a woman who doesn't even want my ass."

Keyton looked at me. "Damn, I didn't know it was like that. I mean, I knew you had it bad, but damn, no pussy in weeks. I would need to be checked into a fucking rehabilitation center. PA: Pussy Anonymous or some shit." He laughed.

"This shit funny to you?"

"Vagina Withdrawals Support Group."

I laughed at his ass. "Yo, I'm out. I ain't feeling this shit tonight," I said, dapping him up.

"Wait, you gon' leave yo' girl here with all these vultures?"

I grabbed my coat off the rack in the corner. "She ain't mines, man. She too good for the kid, but that's cool. I'm 'bout to go find me a hood bitch to suck my dick."

Key walked toward the elevator with me. "Nia gon' kill yo' ass. I can't do a hood bitch, man. In fact, I'm about to go dance with my wife before she gets any ideas."

We both turned to leave the office until the desk phone rang. We looked at each other then at the phone for a moment before we walked over to the desk. That phone was strictly business and almost never rang unless some shit had popped off. I walked over and picked it up through the speaker.

"Yeah," I said as I adjusted my jacket.

"We got some shit to take care of," Marco said through the phone. "I had a run-in with Top, the little nigga who used to run with Flacco. Apparently, niggas heard we were clearing house and got some shit with them. We need to get in front of this shit before it gets messy."

I shook my head as I let what Marco had just said process. This shit was a never-ending cycle of bullshit. I couldn't get out of the game without niggas trying to keep me there. Yet, at the same time, they hated a nigga because I took from them when I ate. I promised my mother that I was getting out, and wasn't shit changing that. I needed to follow through with this shit, and I needed Key with me.

"How the fuck this Flacco shit keep coming back to haunt us?" Key asked, rubbing his chin. "Come to the office."

"I'm almost there," Marco said, disconnecting the call.

I looked up at Key and knew he was stressing about this shit. The last time we tried to make this type of move, it almost cost Tori her life. I knew he wasn't trying to go down that road again, and hell, I wasn't either.

"Don't trip on this shit, man. We don't know all the details yet."

He looked at me. "I can't deal with this shit right now. We have to finish this hotel. The opening is in two months. Tori and Nia about to graduate, and we have to plan their party. I can't be looking over my shoulder for a nigga trying to off me or my wife."

At that moment, Marco walked in with a mug on his face. I knew Marco well enough to know he was pissed the fuck off and wanted blood. If people knew what Key and I knew about Marco, niggas wouldn't fuck with him. I was once on the other end of his wrath, and I thanked God that now we were like brothers.

"I ain't feeling this shit, man," Marco said, walking up to us. "That little nigga Top almost got bodied for being the fucking messenger!"

I shook my head. This shit was crazy already. "Where you run into this nigga at?"

"He was at the store around the corner from Lennox. I just got through checking the spot and was heading to get an update on the hotel when he flagged me down. We have to lock this shit down. Like now!"

I nodded. "I feel you on that! We have to get ahead of it. Immediately."

"I'll put some ears to the street. See what people saying," Marco said, standing up and looking down at the club. "I just gotta know who we dealing with."

"Yeah, I feel that," Key said, nodding.

"What the fuck?" Marco whispered. "How the hell she gon' tell me she busy but be up in the fucking club, bruh?"

"Yeah, I just saw that. I'm about to go snatch Tori little ass up now. You coming with me?"

Marco shook his head. "I can't deal with Winter ass right now. I'm about to go make a call to the contractor to make sure they at the hotel next week when we stop by. Y'all still rolling, right?"

"Of course," I said, dapping Marco up. "I'm excited about the hotel, man. Even more excited than I was when we opened the club. So far, it looks good as fuck. I can't wait to get me a buck-naked freak in my top-floor suite and wax that ass on the balcony overlooking the city."

Marco and Key laughed at me as we headed to the elevator.

Chapter 10

TaNia

"You need to stop being so scared, Nia."

I rolled my eyes. Tori could come out of nowhere with some shit. "What are you talking about?" I sipped my vodka cranberry. "Hey, you asked me to come out, so I'm here."

"Yeah, I know what I asked you, but why you do Mon like that? You know he really likes you."

If I had a dollar for every time I heard that . . . "He likes a lot of people."

Tori laughed. "Now you and I both know that ain't true."

"So, you giving Mon a hard time?" Winter asked as she looked at me.

"He is giving his own self a hard time. All he has to do is move on to someone he actually goes well with. That just ain't me."

"But how do you know that, TaNia?" Winter asked.

I smiled as I sipped my drink again. "Because we just don't. I know that for sure. I'm not the type of chick he goes for, Winter. He likes girls who look like you and Tori."

"Shit," Tori said, laughing. "Obviously we don't do it for him because he wants him some TaNia Monae."

Winter laughed as she nodded. "Girls come for him left and right, and he shuts them down like he married or some shit. I don't see why you won't give him a chance."

I smirked when I saw Keyton make his way through the crowd to us. I knew he would be coming sooner or later. I low-key wanted Mon to be with him when he did.

Tori sipped her drink and smiled. "His cologne fucks up my senses every time."

I chuckled as she turned to him.

"What's up, sexy? You got a man?" he teased.

She laughed as she turned back to us. "Fuck no! I'm single!"

Keyton looked like he wanted to strangle her, and I couldn't contain my laughter. He stepped in front of her. "Oh that's funny, Winter and Nia?" he said, looking at me. "Aye, Tonya," he said, calling one of the bartenders. "No more drinks on the house for these three. Charge they ass regular customer price, and water they shit all the way down, too."

"Oh, hell no," Winter said, laughing. "He said water our drinks down, though?"

"That's messed up." I was barely able to get it out because I was laughing so hard. "This dude said regular customer price!"

"Y'all some regular chicks tonight, hell. Fuck all that, though," he said, looking at Tori. "You look good as fuck!" He grabbed her by her waist and pulled her to him. They were so in love it made me sick. I just sipped my drink and looked on while he wrapped his arms around her. "I need to have a very important discussion with you in my office regarding a very serious matter."

Tori bit her bottom lip. "How serious?"

Keyton grabbed her hand and pulled it in front of him. From where I stood, it looked like he placed it on his dick. The way Tori looked at him confirmed my suspicion. "These fools about to get down right in front of me," I whispered below the music.

"I need a fucking man," Winter said in an agitated voice.

"It's like level-ten, top-notch G14 classified!" His face was so serious it was hilarious. "Like this shit is of high importance, Tori!"

Winter and I were dying laughing at this point! This dude made going to his office and having sex sound like World War III.

"I can't leave Nia and Winter down here alone, Key. What my girls gon' do while I go save the world?"

Keyton turned to me. "You need to go find Mon. That nigga said he was leaving 'cause you tripping." He then turned to Winter and laughed when Marco walked up behind her.

"This why you too busy for me?" Marco said, scaring the shit out of Winter.

"What the hell, Demarco. I almost spilled my drink. Make some noise next time."

"We in a loud-ass club, Winter. Fuck is you scared for?"

She turned to him and tried her hardest not to smile. I had no idea they were even talking. Marco was a great guy with a rough past. He was super attractive, but I couldn't recall him ever talking to anyone. It was weird to see him take an interest in Winter.

"You creeping up behind me ain't cool, Demarco."

"She gets to call you Demarco?" Tori said, smiling. "I try that shit and you ice grill the hell outta me."

"He don't even let me call him that and I'm his best friend," Key said, smiling.

Marco frowned as he grabbed Winter's arm. "Let me talk to you really quick," he said, pulling her away from us.

"Bye, y'all," she said, giggling as she disappeared into the crowd.

I laughed as I turned back to Key. "How am I tripping?"

"Come on, Nia. You stay curving that nigga. He ain't used to that shit. He feeling you. Has been for a minute, and you just brush him off like he doesn't matter."

Damn, I'd never looked at it like that. He could have had any girl he wanted. I had been so stuck on the idea that I felt I didn't deserve him to realize that he could have any girl, even multiple girls at the same time. But he wanted me. Just me.

"Where is he?" I asked Key as he groped Tori's ass and kissed her neck. He didn't even hear me speak. "Key, where is Mon?"

He released Tori partially and turned to me. "He pro'ly is leaving out the back."

I nodded. "All right, Tor, I'm gon' catch you later. Call me."

"Wait, you want me to walk you?"

"Hell no!" Key spat before he knew it. "Baby, come on. Damn," he whined. He grabbed his phone from his pocket. "Ay, Cortez, come get Nia. Take her to Mon for me."

"Nigga, you ain't passing my friend off to the fucking help!" Tori said, grabbing his phone.

"Cancel that shit, Cortez!" She hung up before she gave him his phone back.

Keyton looked at her. "Damn, Tori. Chill the fuck out!"

"I'm walking you," Tori said, looking at me and escaping Keyton's grasp.

"I can just walk my damn self," I said, grabbing my phone out of my clutch. I dialed Mon.

"Yo!" he answered, his voice slurred, clearly drunk.

"Where are you?"

He laughed before he spoke. "Getting my dick sucked!"

I almost dropped my phone out of my hand. "Are you fucking serious?"

"Dead ass!"

I hung up the phone. I felt myself about to hyperventilate. "I'm gon' need bail money, Tor."

"What the fuck? Why?" She had the most confused expression on her face.

I was beyond pissed off. "This bitch just told me he was getting his dick sucked. I'm about to kill him and that ho!"

Tori looked genuinely lost and perplexed. "What the hell?"

I looked at Keyton, who just held his head down. "Where the fuck he park at, Key?"

Keyton had a dumb look on his face before Tori turned to him. "Fuck this nigga at, Key?" she asked.

Keyton looked down at Tori and smiled. "I'on know." He shrugged.

"You lying!" Tori got in his face.

Keyton looked like he was about to pounce on her ass. He smiled and licked his lips. I wasn't sure why, but he wanted him some Tori, like right now. "You better move yo' sexy ass back up out my face. I'm liable to bite yo' ass!"

Tori didn't back down. "Just know I bite back, and stop lying! Where he at, Key?"

"I don't know, Tori. He said he was out and that was it."

"Call him."

I smirked when I saw Keyton's smile drop. He was gon' do whatever he had to do to stay on her good side. "Damn, Tori."

"Key," she said, looking at him. She got closer to him and lowered her voice. "This situation we need to take care of can't wait. You know that G14 classified shit we got to deal with? Well, before I can handle that, I need you to locate Mon."

It was like she had this dude hypnotized. Keyton grabbed his phone out of his pocket and called Mon.

"Speakerphone," I whispered.

Keyton looked at me like I was crazy. "This shit all the way against the code."

"Fuck the code," I said, annoyed.

Mon's phone rung for a moment before he answered. "Yo! This better be important, nigga!"

Keyton shook his head. "I need you to come back to the office."

"The fuck for? Some shit went down?"

Keyton ran his hand down his waves. "You can say that."

"Yo, if this shit is not important, I'm really needed where I'm at!"

"Where is he?" I whispered.

Keyton looked at me for a minute, then he turned to Tori, who glanced at her watch. I watched Keyton's eyes slide over her body before they landed on her face. He was literally obsessed with her. So much so that he was about to sell out his main man. "Where you at?"

"I'm parked in the back," he slurred.

That wasn't far at all, and it was all I needed to hear. I took off speed walking with Tori right behind me. I was almost to the back door when he came through it with some skinny chick with a bad sew-in. She was all over him, and all I saw was red. "You fucking with lames now, Mon?"

He looked up and shook his head. He knew me well enough to know I was pissed. "Say, don't start, Nia."

"Fuck you!" I walked up to him, not giving a damn about her. "What, 'cause this bitch sucked ya dick you in love or whatever?

Mon released the girl, who hadn't said shit. *Good idea, bitch!*

"Fuck you tight for, Nia?"

I looked at him like he was crazy. "You just had a dude escorted out for speaking to me, Lemonte! But it's okay for you to get your dick sucked?"

"Fuck yeah. You know why? 'Cause I'm done chasing you. I ain't no fucking bum-ass dude. I can get pussy!"

The bitch beside him giggled. I looked at her sideways for a minute. The silence around us was still. You could hear a pin drop in a crowded club. "Something funny?"

She waved her hands in front of her. "Look, this ain't got shit to do with me."

Keyton held Tori around her waist. He knew if I went in, she was going too. I guessed he wasn't trying to see that happen. Tori laughed as she spoke. "Realest shit I heard all night, so step ya ass off!"

She looked at Tori in her moment of hesitation before she walked off, leaving only us four in the small hallway.

"Tell me you're drunk, Lemonte!" I was on the verge of hitting him dead in that fucking dimple he got. "That's the only reason you would do some dumb shit like this!"

He looked at me and licked his lips. The fact that he just got done letting that ugly bitch suck his dick was bothering me more than it should have. The sudden need to get away from him became present. I continued to look at him, waiting for him to respond to my question. "Are you going to answer me?"

His eyes told me that he was debating whether he should answer. Then he spoke. "You fucking dissed my ass. You had a dude in your face! Then you hung up on me! I wasn't feeling that shit! Like I said, I been chasing you too long, and it's a dead fucking end. I get it! I'm done. On to the next!"

I wouldn't lie and say I wasn't hurt, because I was. I wasn't sure when all these feelings started, but I knew they were there in full force. I was not going to sit here and let him know what his words did to me. So I walked off. "Please don't follow me, Tor. I'll take a cab home."

I knew Tori wasn't having that. "No, the fuck you not, Nia. You rode with me, so I'll take you home."

I heard Keyton grunt. "Say, Mon, take Nia home."

"I'm not getting in the car with his ass."

Mon had this smirk on his face that made my flesh crawl. I was getting more pissed by the minute. I felt like he was mocking me. Like he didn't care that I was clearly upset. He was like all the other childish motherfuckers I'd dealt with. "I don't give a fuck, Nia."

He shouldn't have said shit to me. I dropped my purse so quick and was on his ass. My heels made me almost eye level with him, but it was still clear he was taller than me. I didn't give a fuck, though. He blocked most of them, but I was able to land a few punches, swinging blow after blow as hard as I could until I felt strong arms wrap around me and lift me off my feet effortlessly.

"Aye, you gon' make me fuck you up, Nia. Don't put your fucking hands on me, man!"

I was crying at this point, pissed off for letting his ass get to me. I had to keep asking myself the question why. "I swear I hate you! On to the next, my nigga? Cool! Don't call me! Don't text! None of that shit, Lemonte! Let me go, Keyton!"

"I can't do that," Keyton said, still holding me back.

"Nia, calm down," Tori said, pleading with me.

"I'm so done, Lemonte! If you wanted to play games, you could have played them with somebody else!"

Chapter 11

Lemonte

I couldn't believe she swung on me! I was still in shock, no lie. I didn't know she cared. I thought all this curving she was doing was because she didn't want me. In fact, she did say that to me in so many words. So to say I was thrown off by how pissed off she was would be an understatement. "I never once played with you, Nia. I have been chasing you for years!"

"Whatever! Like I said, I'm done. I'm leaving!"

She was still trying to get away from Key. "Let her go, man."

Key let her go, and she grabbed her purse. "Tori, please don't follow me!"

"She ain't got to follow you, because I'm taking you home."

She turned to me. "No, you not!"

I leaned forward to get in her face. "Who the fuck gon' stop me?"

Tori looked at Nia. "I'm not letting you catch a cab, Nia. That's not going down."

She was still crying, and it was slowly killing me knowing I caused those tears. I didn't want to hurt her. I didn't know how this happened so fast, but I knew I wanted to fix it. "I'll take you home, Nia. You don't have to say anything to me. I will just make sure you get home."

She wiped her tears with her hand and looked up at me. "Fine," she mumbled as she walked out the door.

The three of us stood in the hallway for a moment not saying anything.

Tori broke the silence. "She has been my friend for ten years, and I have not once seen her act like that. She never cries, and she sure as hell does not swing on people. I'm shocked!"

"Shit, me too!" Key said, smiling and shaking his head. "She clocked yo' ass, too! Shit was too funny! Her ass may not fight often, but she damn sure know how!"

"You have to be patient with her, Mon. She been through a lot and her trust is fucked up. She needs a certain level of understanding," said Tori.

I felt like shit. It wasn't my intent to hurt Nia. Never that.

"Take care of my girl," Tori said, hugging me. "She cares a lot!"

"I got her, Tori."

She smiled at me. "I know."

I walked out the door to see Nia leaned up against my car. She stood straight when I approached.

"That bitch suck ya dick in here, Mon? I'm not getting in this car if she did! Don't lie!"

I stopped short in front of her. "That bitch didn't suck my dick, man. I just told you that shit!"

She shook her head and threw her hands up dramatically. "But you don't play games, though, right?"

She folded her arms over her chest and looked away from me. I could kick my own ass at this point. "Look, Nia. I'm sorry, all right? I didn't mean to upset you."

She sucked her teeth and twisted her lips. "Ha! Telling me a bitch sucked your dick would be the thing to piss me off!"

"I didn't know you cared enough for it to matter! You don't want a relationship with me outside of friendship, so why do you care?"

She looked down at her feet and bit into her bottom lip. She was nervous. "I care, Lemonte, but I'm scared."

Now I was really confused. "Scared of what? Scared of me?"

"Of this!" she half yelled, pointing between the two of us. "I'm out here crying and fighting and we not even together! I've been played with, and I'm tired of that! All I do is go to school and work. I make sure my mom is good, and I keep my head down. Why? Because I want to be missed off the bullshit. I want my peace, and being with you would disrupt that!"

I stepped closer to her, pinning her against my car. She still held her head down. I got the feeling there was way more there than what I saw on the surface. She was hiding something. I wanted to know what. "Tell me, Nia. What's the deal? Talk to me."

She ran her hand down her arm then wiped her face again before more tears could fall. "I'm not the woman for you. That's all."

I placed my hand under her chin so that she could look into my eyes, and that's when I saw it. Insecurity. I had absolutely no idea how she could be insecure being that she was beautiful, but she was. I needed to do all I could to make her feel secure with me and ensure that she did all she had to do to feel secure in herself.

"You know how beautiful you are?"

She smirked and rolled her eyes. "Come on, Lemonte. I've seen you with prettier girls!"

I laughed at that shit. She had no idea. "Those girls be fake, Nia. Fake ass, fake breasts, fake hair. Fake eyes, lashes, fake everything. You use those types of chicks for one thing and one thing only. I would never wife none of them type of women. They just look good. They don't mold against my body like a real woman. I need someone soft and warm." I licked my lips and ran my eyes over her. "Someone like you, Nia. Something real! Your skin, your eyes, your lips, the fact that you have your own hair and the weave is optional. I want Nia!" I looked into her eyes. "Shit, not once have I taken any of them hoes seriously. I've always known the one I wanted. She just keeps shutting me down!"

She licked her lips. "She didn't want to get hurt. She doesn't want to get hurt."

I smiled at the fact that she was knowingly speaking about herself in the third person. "I would never hurt her. She should know that!"

"Will you respect her? Stay truthful, never lie, never cheat?"

I held my hand up like I was pledging allegiance because in a sense I was. "I solemnly swear to take care of Nia's heart. Respect her mind."

She smiled up at me, and I smiled back. "And my body?"

I stepped back to look down at her. I had to take a deep breath. This was what a real woman looked like. Big, full, natural breasts, a curved waistline with thick, round hips, and a thick ass. A perfect hourglass. Perfection.

I licked my lips and smiled. "What about that mutherfucka?" I asked, causing her to laugh.

After a moment of laughing, she looked me in my eyes again, connecting to my soul. "It's not too much for you?"

I couldn't stop the frown that covered my face. "What the fuck? Hell no! Nia. Your body is perfect, baby!"

"That's because you haven't seen me with my clothes off," she whispered.

A wicked smiled covered my face as I unlocked my car. "We can fix that."

She looked at me for a moment, possibly trying to see how serious I was. "Really?"

"Dead ass," I said, nodding. "It doesn't matter to me. Here, my place, a room. I'll take all your clothes off and get a better look."

She laughed as she pushed her braids to the back. My heart skipped a beat.

"I would much rather have you laugh around me then cry. That shit is my kryptonite, Nia. I almost cried because you were crying."

She laughed again. I smiled, exhaling a breath I wasn't aware I was holding. "Forgive me, baby. Give me a chance. I want you to be mine."

She exhaled and held her head back before she looked at me. I walked back up to her. "Please, Lemonte! Just don't hurt me. Promise me you won't hurt me."

I kissed her forehead and hugged her. "I promise you, Nia. You in good hands with Allstate."

She laughed again and nodded. "Okay. But if you hurt me, I'm fucking you up! I got a crazy best friend, too. She ready for whatever."

"Oh, I know," I said, kissing her hand. "I don't want no problems. You already done swung on me. Little violent self!"

She flushed in embarrassment. "I don't know what came over me. I'm sorry for that."

"You good, baby!"

"Okay," she whispered. She looked back up at me and ran her free hand over my dreads. Her lips looked so welcoming, so I accepted the invitation.

She was hesitant at first, as if she didn't know what to do with me kissing her. But after a moment, I felt her lips soften under mine, and she was kissing me back. I pressed my body to hers and swallowed her moan as she opened up more. She tasted so good. I knew she would. She wrapped her arms around my neck as I grabbed her waist and slid my tongue down her throat. She whimpered against my lips. She had this certain innocence about her as if she wasn't used to being with a man in this manner. Maybe she was just nervous. Yeah, that was it.

It seemed like we were kissing forever. Forget breathing. She was enough air. I was on cloud nine. It was a crazy night, but I finally got the girl of my dreams on my team.

Chapter 12

Keyton

It was time to get back on it. I had been slipping as a husband because, simply put, I had too much shit going on between the club and the restaurants. Plus, me, Marco, and Mon just started making moves to open a hotel in downtown Dallas. Downtown was the perfect place, and it just so happened that the perfect property had become available a little over a year ago. I jumped on that like white on rice.

I kept looking at some pictures, wondering what the fuck it all meant. I wasn't one to jump the gun, but something was off. The unmarked van was in every single picture. Every one of them. The other common denominator was that either my wife, TaNia, or Winter was there, too. Since the first time some shit went down, I wasn't taking any risks. Tori, being the super stubborn, independent woman she was, would not accept detailed security while she was out. She wanted to do things her own way and in her own time. So, I still assigned security, she just didn't know he was there. After Mon had started kicking it heavy with Nia, he ordered the same service for her. Same thing with Marco.

"I thought we buried this shit, Key," Marco said, looking at me with murder in his eyes.

I exhaled as I shook my head. "I thought the same thing, man. I don't know why the fuck they keep coming back," I yelled. I felt myself get frustrated. "The thing about these wack mother-fuckers is that they don't come at me. They fuck with Tori because they know she all I fucking got. I ain't dealing with this shit, man!"

Marco looked at me and knew I was beyond pissed off! Tori and I had enough pulling us apart. We didn't need all this added shit!

"We'll handle it," Marco said, nodding.

"My marriage can't take another blow, Marco. She already can't stand my ass and wants to leave. I'm starting to think I'm more harm to her than good."

"Come on, Key. Don't say shit like that. That woman loves you."

I shook my head as I sat down. "She has been through so much shit," I said as I held my head down. "Fuck!"

I heard the door open and knew it was Mon. He had been on cloud nine lately being that Nia is giving him the time of day. I hated to be the one to ruin his shit. I knew if those bitch niggas were going for Tori, they would be going for Nia and Winter as well. Being that they were in the pictures as well, I knew this shit was bigger than we thought. The fact that we hadn't had any situations with any of the spots or businesses let me know that the people behind this were on some personal shit.

"What's the play?" he said, lying across the couch on the opposite side of my office.

I looked at him at the same time that Marco did, and he immediately recognized that something wasn't right. "What's up?" he asked, sitting up.

I passed Marco the pictures and watched as he passed them to Mon. Mon looked at the pictures for a moment before he exploded.

"Yo, why the fuck these niggas keep coming for us?" he yelled, throwing the pictures down. "Where the fuck they come from?" Mon never yelled, so to say he was pissed would be an understatement.

"I think this has to do with us pulling out the game. This can't be the same niggas from last year," Marco said as he stood. "Remember that shit I told you Top was spitting?"

"You think this got something to do with Flacco?" Mon asked. "We barely had shit to do with Flacco."

"What the fuck that got to do with us? We are getting out this shit, Marco. Niggas should be fucking toasting to that," I said, pissed off.

"But he had sons, Key. I know the Cartel did the job, but everybody in his fucking camp got bodied but you two. Everybody knows who the fuck I am and what I do. They know I was the biggest hit man for the Cartel. Now we make money together. I feel like I'm bringing this shit to y'all front door."

I could look at Marco and tell this shit was bothering him. "We are fucking brothers, Marco. I don't give a fuck about how nobody feels! We will handle this together."

"But now they are following Tori, Nia, and Winter. We don't know who the hell these niggas are. Top just said the shit was somehow connected to Flacco. We still don't know shit."

"What the fuck does that matter?" I asked, frustrated.

"They may be on some revenge-type shit."

I took a moment to think about that shit. That went down when I was a fucking kid. I didn't recall him ever speaking of any family, but I was just a runner. I didn't have any type of position of power when that shit was going on. I was just trying to protect the people I loved. I didn't snitch or roll over on nobody. Flacco fucked his own shit up being greedy and wanting shit we didn't need. He was a fucking millionaire. That was all I needed. Being that I had successfully reached that point, my team and I were gracefully bowing out.

"So, who telling the ladies they on lockdown until this shit over?" That question came from Mon.

"Man, Tori is not going to wanna hear that noise. Y'all know how she is. 'Really, Key,'" I said, mocking her. "'You want me to stay in the house while you run around doing you? What part of the game that is?'" I laughed at myself as I grabbed my blunt and lit it.

"No, bro," Mon said, laughing. "Nia ass," he said, shaking his head. "'Ummm, Mon, I ain't doing it! Nope! I got work! I got school! I got shit to do!'"

I laughed hard as hell as I passed Marco the blunt.

"Trying to tell Winter what to do is like pulling teeth, man. She ain't going down without a fight. I'm trying to get her to stop dancing. She won't do that! But I'm gon' put it to her like this: I want her to manage the hotel. She about to graduate, she going to need something fast, and with Nia and Tori working there too, I think she may roll with it."

"That's a good idea, Marco. They all have business degrees in some way. I hope that works for you. I'll have Tori drop a bug in her ear."

"I'll talk to TaNia too."

"But look I was thinking. With it getting hot around here, maybe we should take them on vacation. Somewhere warm!" I suggested as I grabbed my bottled water and took a swig.

"That's a good idea," Marco said. "I need to teach Winter ass how to shoot. She saw my gun in the glove compartment the other day and almost pissed on herself. I got so many of them muthafuckas, I forget where I leave them. Wherever we go, I need to find a range."

"Tori learned to shoot last year. She got a nine she won't leave the house without."

"TaNia knows a little something. She needs a gun, though."

"Well, let's get the conversation out the way, and then we'll go from there."

"Cool," Marco said as he stood. We all dapped up before we left the office.

Chapter 13

Demarco

I looked down at the blueprint for the site and couldn't contain my smile. I couldn't believe we had a few weeks until opening and this was going to be partially my hotel. I went from having nowhere to sleep to being part owner of a hotel that I knew would be a success. It was still very surreal.

"This is hot," Winter said, leaning against the wall. "I get to stay with you right, in the penthouse suite?"

I brought my eyes up to look at her. She was dressed down and still killing shit. She had her long, natural hair pulled back into a ponytail, and she had no makeup on. Her jeans rode low on her hips, and her tank top showed her belly button piercing. We had been kicking it for about four months now, and so far I was feeling her. I had to admit it was scary to have feelings for her so soon, but she had this pull about her that I couldn't explain or fight against for that matter. She was so different from any girl I'd ever met. She had goals she wouldn't let me get in the way of. She had opinions and thoughts that she wanted me to listen to and wouldn't come off the topic until I did just that. We did things in her time. Anything other than that was straight bullshit. Right now the only issue we had was her occupation. Don't get me wrong, I wasn't judging her because she worked at the club. I just didn't want her doing it anymore. The first fifty times I expressed that, she shut me down. She wasn't trying to hear shit I was talking about.

I didn't reply to her and just looked back down at the blueprints. Until she would at least entertain the conversation, I was trying to guard my heart against her. The last thing I needed was to fall for her only for her to choose that lifestyle over me. I may sound weak, but I didn't give a fuck. My future wife didn't belong in the club shaking her ass while I could take care of her. I leaned up against the wall opposite her as I continued to look down.

She got a message on her phone that caused me to look up at her. I saw her roll her eyes and stuff her phone back into her back pocket, and I knew it had to be that fuck boy she used to be with.

"Say, you gon' get your number changed anytime soon?"

"What?" she said, looking confused.

"I'm saying I don't like the fact that he still has your number. Any of them old niggas, for that matter."

She smirked as she pulled her phone out. "How do you know it was him?"

I looked into her beautiful eyes and lost my train of thought. "Just get your number changed, Winter."

I smelled her perfume as she walked closer to me. "You mad?"

"Nah, ma, you good," I said, halfway paying attention.

She leaned into me and kissed my cheek. "Why you ignoring me then?"

"I'm not ignoring you, Winter," I said.

She kissed my neck and pressed her body against me, standing between my legs. She stood up on her tiptoes and kissed my lips, not caring that she was destroying my blueprints. If I was honest, I didn't give a fuck either.

"Stop being mean," she said against my lips.

"I'm not," I mumbled as I kissed her back. I couldn't resist this woman. She had me hooked already.

"You are, Demarco," she said as she ran her hand down my chest. There was something about the way she said my name that immediately made my dick hard.

"You better stop kissing me like that before I pin yo' ass up against this wall," I said, smiling down at her.

"Really?" she said, still kissing. "You promise, Demarco?"

Her voice alone had me actually considering that shit even though we were in crowded-ass downtown. "Quit playing with me, Winter," I said, frowning down at her.

She poked her lips out and wrinkled her nose at me. She took a few steps back and let her eyes move down me. She was the biggest tease, man. She was all talk and no action. You would think I was the side dude or some shit the way she was holding out.

"You are no fun," she said, fake pouting.

I shook my head as we walked back into the hotel. We had a few final touches to make before the grand opening, but it wasn't anything that would set us back. I was giving it three months before Three Kings would be in business.

I felt Winter move up behind me and wrap her arms around my waist as best she could as I looked around the lobby. "This is such a blessing! I'm so happy for you," she said against my lower back. Her short ass.

"Thank you," I said, looking around. I turned around to face her. Even with the workers and foreman running around behind us, I could only hear and feel her. I hoped she didn't flip out on me with the next statement I was about to make. She had in the past, and I didn't feel like going through that shit again.

"So, I need you to lie low for a little bit. I mean, you could move in with me for a minute, which would be perfect, but—"

"Wait," Winter said, holding her hands up. "Lie low? Move in? Demarco, you're taking too fast. What are you talking about?"

"I need you to move in with me."

"But why?"

"You're being followed," I said nonchalantly as I began to look back at the blueprints.

"Being followed?" she almost yelled out.

"Yes, Winter, and I need to make sure you're safe at all times. So once you graduate next month, I'll need a few things from you."

"A few things like what?"

"I don't want you to strip at the club anymore, Winter."

She didn't respond immediately. She just stood there looking at me. After a while, she released me and wrapped her arms around her waist. "Don't do this, Demarco."

"Do what?" I asked, frowning down at her. "I'm serious, Winter. I want you to stop."

"We've had this conversation a million times, and I know that you're serious, but I can't do that. I'm sorry."

"What the fuck you mean you can't do it?" I growled, looking down at her. "I don't give a shit! That's my club!"

"So you gon' fire me for no reason?" She was pissed and almost yelling, but I didn't give a fuck.

"That pretty much sums it up. I don't want to argue with you—"

"And we won't," she said, cutting me off. "I'll just work at another club."

She went to storm off, and I grabbed her. "No, the fuck you won't, Winter," I growled through clenched teeth. "Stop fucking with me."

"Let me go," she yelled as she snatched away from me. She walked to the car where the driver waited to take us to our next destination.

I exhaled deeply as I followed her. I knew this conversation wasn't going to go over smoothly, but I didn't think she would flip out on me. When I got inside, she was pressed as far into the opposite corner of the back seat as she could go. I laughed as I watched her pout as she scrolled through her phone.

"I wish I had my car. I wouldn't be in here wit'cho selfish self," she said, not looking up at me.

"How am I selfish, baby girl? Because I don't want my woman shaking her ass for different dudes every night?"

"You knew what it was before we got together, Demarco. I don't know why you thought anything would change. I still have bills and tuition I have to take care of, and don't even start with that 'I can take care of you' bull crap, because I'm not doing that again."

"Say," I said, annoyed. "Don't ever compare me to that fuck dude you were with. I'm nothing like him. If I say I'm going to make sure you straight, then I'll make sure you straight. So when I say quit, you don't have to worry about me ever saying shit about what I do for you."

She exhaled deeply and rolled her eyes. "It's not about you, Demarco. It's about me!"

I looked at her, confused as hell. "But you just said—"

"Look," she said, waving her hand as she cut me off, "I won't be depending on a man to take care of me. I did that already, and I'm not doing it again. So, I'm not quitting my job. If I'm being followed I know it has to do with some shit you in, but I can't lie low, and I can't move in with you. Either you can deal with it or move around. It's sad because I let my guard down with you. I thought you understood and was cool with it, but I see now that you not man enough to deal with me."

I leaned back in my seat, listening to her spit a whole lot of bullshit, and I honestly wasn't trying to hear any of it. If she felt like she needed to strip, then she could do just that. I didn't have time to deal with it. I had people trying to take me out, I had to get this hotel opened, and I couldn't deal with Winter.

"Take her home," I told the driver as I rattled off her address. She looked at me with hurt flashing in her eyes as he pulled off.

The ride to her house was quiet. Both of us had so much to say but didn't speak anything at all. I wanted her to know that no matter what I had her back and that she would never want or have to work for anything. But because of the mistakes that the little boy before me made, she couldn't trust me. It was fucked up, but it was life. The first woman I ever cared about was a fucking stripper who didn't want to change that for me. Crazy.

We pulled up at her apartment, and she jumped out of the car. I watched her walk behind the car, wiping tears from her eyes. I didn't know why she was crying, and I wanted to just drive off and not care so much, but I couldn't.

I grabbed a note out my pocket and tipped the driver before I got out of the car. I grabbed the bags she left and headed up the stairs. When I made it to her door, it was open, so I let myself in and locked it behind me.

I heard her slamming things around in the kitchen and couldn't help but laugh. She was so used to getting her way and not answering to anyone that she didn't know how to take someone telling her what to do. But she was gon' have to get with the program, because I wasn't having it any other way.

"Get your ass in here," I yelled, throwing her bags on the couch.

She came from around the corner, mean mugging the hell out of me. "I don't know why you're here. I'm not going to stop dancing, and I won't stop my routine because of some shit you in, so we might as well call it quits now."

"Call it quits now," I said, mocking her. "You ain't going nowhere," I murmured, getting in her face. "Ever."

She looked like she was about to slap me. "If you can't accept my job and the fact that I make my own moves, then I won't have a choice."

"What I say goes," I said, pulling her into me. "I'm daddy, girl."

She tried her hardest not to, but she burst out laughing, her dimple showing and her smile melting my heart. "I promise I can't stand you," she said, punching me.

"Ouch," I said, pretending like her little punch hurt. I grabbed her and wrapped my arms around her waist. For a minute, I just looked into her gray eyes and pushed her hair from her face. "I need you to quit, baby. I need a manager for the hotel and you about to graduate. You'll have a degree in accounting as well as business management. Tori and TaNia are on board. Now we just need you. We can move in here or my place, whichever you prefer." I threw that out there in hopes that she would accept the offer. We really did need a manager.

"Are you making shit up, Demarco?" she asked, looking at me.

"Nope," I said, kissing her lips. "So, will you?"

She narrowed her eyes and looked at me suspiciously before she spoke. "Can I think about it?"

I didn't like that shit, but I couldn't push the topic. "Yes."

She smiled as she stood on her tiptoes to kiss me. She wrapped her arms around my neck and pulled up on me. "Short ass," I said as I picked her up. She wrapped her legs around my waist and continued kissing me.

"So," she said, still kissing me. "You taller than Dikembe Mutombo, but you talking, though."

I laughed as I began to walk down the hall to her bedroom. "I ain't taller than that dude, girl. You like it, though."

"I love it," she confessed as she kept kissing me.

Love. That word was difficult for me to process, and I honestly wouldn't know if and when I ever felt it. I never had anyone in my life to feel it for, but I couldn't lie and say I didn't care deeply for Winter.

When we made it to her bedroom, I laid her on the bed and moved on top of her, careful not to smash her under my large frame. Her breasts pressed against my chest as she slid her tongue into my mouth. I kissed her back passionately as I felt her hands reach to my pants to unbuckle my belt buckle. I grabbed her hand to stop her.

Chapter 14

Winter

I looked up into his eyes and saw him, just Demarco. His guard was down, and I knew he wanted exactly what I did. Yes, I had my apprehensions about this relationship, but I knew that I loved him. I knew that I needed him in my life, and I knew that he would protect me. Being around his fine ass and not jumping his bones had been hard these last four months, but I was ready. I wanted him to make love to me.

"You sure, Winter?"

I nodded as I licked my lips. "Yes, baby. I want you to make love to me."

He kissed me again as he released my hands. I immediately returned to the task of taking his belt off.

I looked into his eyes as he moved up to take his shirt off. My eyes automatically moved to his chest, covered in tattoos. He was in perfect shape, and I knew I was looking at him like a main course I was about to devour.

"I want you so much," I moaned as he moved back down to kiss me. I felt his dick resting against my thigh as he reached down and began removing my clothes. His eyes never left mine. His intense stare was making me even more nervous than I already was. "Why are you looking at me like that?" I asked nervously as I ran my fingertips over his stomach.

He smiled at me and kissed my chin. "I'm a lucky man. You're fucking beautiful."

I smiled back as he returned to kissing me. He removed the rest of his clothes quickly before he leaned back to look down at me. "So you know this makes you mines, right? I won't think twice about fucking a nigga up if you give my pussy away."

I rolled my eyes and twisted my lips up. "Yeah, yeah, yeah," I said sarcastically.

He looked at me for a moment. "You're mine."

I nodded. "I am. Are you willing to give me all of you? Mind, body, and soul?"

"In exchange for what?"

"Me," I spoke in a soft voice.

"If I get you, I'll do whatever I have to, Winter."

"You promise me?"

He placed his hand over his heart. "I promise."

"You gon' give me this?" I asked, placing my hand over his heart.

He licked his sexy-ass lips and nodded. "You gon' play with it, Winter?"

"I haven't played with it yet, Demarco," I said seductively as I reached for his manhood. He kissed my lips as he began moving downward. He planted kisses down the center of my body all the way to my pussy. He grabbed my legs and pushed them apart before he started devouring me as if I were the last meal he would ever consume.

"Oh fuck, Demarco," I moaned.

My mind wasn't prepared for what he was doing to me. My thighs shook uncontrollably as his tongue moved over my clit. My hands moved over the waves in his hair as he created deep waves throughout my body. I felt my orgasm run up my spine, so I gripped the sheets to brace myself and was met with no help. At the last minute, Demarco slid two fingers inside me quickly, only intensifying the pressure building between my legs.

"Shit," I moaned, gripping the sheets tighter and squeezing my eyes shut as my entire body shook, completely out of control.

He moved to the side of me to lie on his back and pulled me on top of him. I was exhausted already, and we'd just started. I never had an orgasm that powerful in my life, though I'd only been with two other people. The first person was fresh out of high school, and it only happened once. Then there was Reggie, who was selfish and wouldn't know how to satisfy a woman with a user's guide and a how-to manual!

I didn't get a chance to see what he was working with, and for a minute I felt like he was trying to hide it. I looked down at Demarco as he grabbed his manhood. I glanced down between us and immediately saw why he was hiding his dick from me.

"Anddd, where the fuck is that going, nigga?" I asked, jumping off of him.

"Shit," he growled, sitting up, his monster pointing at me, ready to ruin my life. "Come on, Winter."

"Fuck no," I said, still standing up on wobbly legs.

He laughed at me as he looked down at his dick. I wanted to say it belonged in its own fucking state.

"Demarco, that can't be normal."

He shook his head. "I can't even count how many times I heard that shit."

"Well," I said, grabbing my robe and sliding it on, "I'm sorry. I can't get with it."

"Man," he said with an annoyed expression. "Take that off, Winter. Quit playing!"

"What am I supposed to do with that, Demarco? I want to be able to walk when this is over." He laughed, but I was dead-ass serious. "I'm only twenty-five. I have an entire life to live."

He got up from the bed, and I couldn't help but let my eyes move over him. He was so perfect, from his skin to his lips to even the dick I would never experience. It was beautiful. I wanted to say eleven inches if not more. Veins ran up and down it, making my mouth water.

"Bring yo' ass and quit playing," he said, grabbing me and pulling me back toward the bed. "I'm not gon' hurt you, Winter. That's why I want you on top of me for the first time."

He sat down on the bed and pulled me on top of him before he moved us both back into the position we were just in. I watched nervously as he grabbed a Magnum to place it over his manhood. He looked up at me and kissed me as he positioned himself at my entrance. I closed my eyes and bit my lip, and my entire body trembled.

"Look at me," he groaned as he moved to push deeper inside me.

I slowly opened my eyes to look at him as he stayed in place, giving my body time to adjust to him. I felt myself become wetter around him, making his entry easier. I leaned forward, pressing my breasts against him as I moved my hips down to accept as much of him as I could. I buried my face in his neck as my moans got louder with every thrust.

"Fuck, Winter," I heard him groan against my cheek as I continued to move on top of him.

He began to shift under me, going faster and deeper with each movement.

"I love you, Demarco," I moaned as I creamed all over his dick.

He leaned back to look into my eyes as he continued to move inside of me. He grabbed a handful of my hair and brought my lips down to his.

"Winter," he groaned as he held my ass still and moved into me faster. He looked down at us before his head fell back. I felt the moment he shifted deeper inside me all the way to my stomach.

The muscles in my stomach tightened as my orgasm grabbed me. I closed my mouth and screamed through it, my hands slipped from my silk sheets, and I wrapped my arms around his neck as my body convulsed. "Damn, Demarco!"

"This my shit," he growled in my ear as I came. "My pussy."

"Yes," I screamed, answering his statement as if it were a question. "Ohhh fuck!"

"Come for me, Winter."

And I did just that, over and over until the sun went away and came back up.

Chapter 15

Lemonte

"My pants too tight! They gon' think I'm some super thot trying to destroy their child's life!"

I looked at TaNia and tried not to laugh out loud at her silly ass. "Man, get out the car, woman. You met them both before!"

She shook her head and remained inside the car, seat belt buckled as if we hadn't made it to my parents' house ten minutes ago. "They met me as TaNia, the classmate, the friend, not the girlfriend."

I smiled at her because this was my first time hearing her refer to herself as my girlfriend. That shit had me on ten.

"What?" she asked nervously. "I hate this outfit. Do you like it, Lemonte? Please don't lie to me."

"Man, I'm about to get Momma to pull you out the car."

"No," she whispered as if they would hear her. She unbuckled her seat belt and got out of the car quick as hell.

"I should've said that ten minutes ago."

"Don't say anything embarrassing, Mon. Please?"

"Something like, 'Ma, TaNia can twerk that ass,'" I said as we walked up the driveway.

TaNia's eyes got big as my mother opened the door.

"She makes all that ass move like a tidal wave," I whispered where only she could hear.

"Please, Mon," she whispered, pleading with her eyes.

"Baby, relax," I said, wrapping my arm around her neck and pulling her closer to me. I kissed her cheek then grabbed her hand.

"Ohhh, look at you two," my mom said, smiling from ear to ear.

"Hey, Ma," I said, kissing her cheek. She hugged me and kissed me back before grabbing TaNia in a bear hug.

"I missed you, young lady."

"I missed you too, Mrs. Porsha," TaNia said, hugging her back. "I should've been to see you a long time ago. I've just been so busy."

"Oh, I understand," Ma said as she pulled TaNia into the house. I slapped her ass as I followed them. She looked back at me like she wanted to kill me.

I stuck my tongue out and kept walking as if nothing happened. Once inside, I went straight to the kitchen. I knew Ma prepared a feast for TaNia, and I was about to reap the benefits. She had everything spread out on the counter: ribs, mac and cheese, mashed potatoes, broccoli, rice and cheese casserole, Hawaiian rolls, and some good ol' Southern diabetic Kool-Aid. "Hell yes," I said, going to wash my hands.

"We ain't eating until your father gets here, Deon. Come out of the kitchen," my mother yelled from the living room. When she called me my middle name, she meant business, so I grudgingly came out of the kitchen.

"Where Pops at, Ma?" I asked in an annoyed tone.

"He says that he is five minutes away," she said, looking back at me. "He can't wait to see you, TaNia. We haven't laid eyes on you since you graduated."

"I know," TaNia said, looking over at me for help. I held my hands up and walked over to sit beside her. "Mon and I just reconnected, honestly. We lost touch for a minute after high school. But, here we are," she said bashfully as she looked at me.

"Yeah, you finally stopped running from my baby," Ma said, smiling. Even though I was twenty-six years old and a boss, I was still just a baby to my mom. I wouldn't fix my mouth to correct her.

After about ten more minutes of chitchat, Pops finally walked in. "Finally," I said, jumping up to hug him. I was happier that I was about to eat than I was to see him. "Pops, what's good wit'chu?"

My dad was possibly the humblest man I ever met. He loved his wife like crazy, and he was a hard worker. All my life Pops worked while my mother tended to the house, but he didn't limit her to just that. Anything she wanted to do within reason, my father allowed her to do. Anything she needed was there for her before she could verbally say it. He loved her unconditionally. Growing up looking up to my Pops made me the man I was today. I wanted to be all that to my future wife and more. I didn't want her to stress or want for anything. I wanted her to be able to take a risk and follow her dreams with me as a safety net. I wanted her to be happy with me and still glance at me with love in her eyes while looking at me even after thirty years of being together, like my mother was looking at my father now.

"Hey, baby," he said, curving me and walking over to my mother, who stood to kiss him.

"I mean, I'm like right here, though," I said, holding my arms up as Nia laughed.

Dad released my mother to turn and look at me. "Who could miss this big head, boy? Get over here!" He pulled me into a bear hug before he released me and hugged TaNia. "How are you, baby girl?" he asked, looking at her with sympathy in his eyes.

She nodded and gave him a weak smile. "I'm okay," she said, half smiling.

"You know you're like a daughter to us, TaNia. If you ever need anything, just let us know. Do you hear me?"

"Yes, sir," TaNia said, smiling.

"So," I said, interrupting their little reunion. "About this food, though."

We all sat at the table as my father said grace. I was surprised that TaNia actually made my plate and served me just as my mother did my father. She wouldn't sit down until I let her know that I didn't need anything else. I was smiling so hard at her, because I thought it was the sexiest shit ever.

Once everything was in place, we all began to eat. "This is so good, Mrs. Porsha," TaNia said, smiling down at my mother. "I remember when I used to make sure Mon was my partner so that we could do class projects together at your house just so I could eat over here. My mom can cook, but she's been on this health kick lately."

"I thought you used to be my partner because I was smart and attractive," I said, smirking at her.

She smiled at me and my heart melted. I knew I was falling in love with TaNia. I could no longer deny that.

"That was part of it," she said as she returned to eating. "But most of it was Mrs. Porsha's cooking."

"I feel so used," I said, covering my heart.

"Thank you, sweetheart," my mother said, smiling. "How is your mother doing?"

TaNia looked down at her food, absently running her fork through her mashed potatoes. "She's good."

"I know that losing your father was hard for her," my dad said. "It's good to hear that she's doing well."

"Yes," TaNia spoke absently. "It was hard for both of us. I moved back in with her after he passed, and now she ready to kick me out."

My mother laughed. "I'm sure that's not true."

"She wants me to stay in the house and not work. The money that dad left when he passed is more than enough for us to live off of and never have to work, but I have to work because you know what the Bible says about an idle mind."

I sat back in my seat and listened to her. We never talked about her dad. It was a topic she curved every chance she got, so to hear her speak of him to my parents was weird.

"It's the devil's playground," my mother said, nodding.

"Yes," TaNia said, smiling.

My dad was leaned back observing her as well, and as soon as we made eye contact, he asked me to step into the den with him.

"Yeah, Pops," I said once he was seated in his lounge chair with me on the love seat across from him.

"I know how you feel about TaNia, Lemonte. How you've always felt. But you're not dealing with the same girl from high school. She's different."

I nodded. "I picked up on that a while ago."

"Does she ever talk about her father to you?"

"Nope," I said, shaking my head. "She dodges the question every time I bring him up, but I know she misses him."

"How is she dealing with it?" he asked me as he grabbed the beer beside him and took a swig.

"That's the thing, Pop. I don't think she does."

"What's different about her, Lemonte?"

The first thing that popped into my head was definitely the drinking. "She drinks more than I do. Most nights, she drinks. It's never excessive until she goes out. That's when she gets drunk off her ass."

He nodded. "Ever ask her why she drinks so much?"

I shook my head no. "I haven't yet, but the more I think about it, I see that's a question I need to ask."

"Deon."

I looked up to see my mother standing in the opening leading to the den. "Yeah, Ma?" I asked, looking up at her.

"TaNia has been in the bathroom for the last ten minutes. I checked on her, and she says she's fine, but she won't come out."

I got up and walked over to my mother. "She in the downstairs one?"

She nodded. "I may have upset her by talking about her dad."

"Don't worry, Ma. I'm sure she's fine."

"Come sit with me, honey," my dad called out to my mom as I walked past her to go to the bathroom Nia was in.

Before I knocked, I leaned into the door and heard her sniffling. "Baby," I said through the door.

"Did I scare your mom, Lemonte?" she asked through her tears. "Tell her that I'm sorry."

I exhaled deeply. "Open the door for me, baby girl."

"I just need a minute."

"Ma said you've been in here for ten. She's worried."

"I'm sorry," she said through the door.

"You want me to kick this door down? Open the door, TaNia."

"Don't please, Lemonte. I'm fine, I promise."

"Well, come out."

After a minute the door opened, and I looked at TaNia, who had clearly been crying her eyes out. "See?" she said with a broken smile.

I pulled her into my arms, and she came willingly. She buried her face in my chest as she sniffled some more before wrapping her arms around me.

"What's the matter, beautiful?" I asked as I gently grabbed her face in my hands so that she could look into my eyes.

She pushed her thick lips together and stood on her tiptoes to kiss me. "I'm fine," she mumbled.

I used my thumbs to wipe the tears from her face. "That's not true, TaNia. Talk to me."

"I need you to sing to me."

I looked down the hall then back at her. "Here?"

"You can sing really low so that I'm the only one who hears you."

I looked down at her and smiled as I ran my thumb over her bottom lip. I sang the first thing that popped into my head: "*Everywhere she go, they playin' my song. That's why I say the things that I say; that way I know you can't ignore me. So gimme all of you in exchange for me. TaNia, give me all of you in exchange for me.*"

She wrapped her arms tighter around me. "You sound amazing. What song is that?"

"Bryson Tiller, 'Exchange,' but of course he didn't say my girl's name."

"Oh, of course not," she said, smiling.

"I need a favor from you," I said, looking at her. "First thing is I need you to move in with me. Not forever if you don't want, but for a little while at least."

"Move in?" she asked, confused.

"Just for a little while," I coaxed. "It wouldn't be long, ma."

"But I have school and work, Mon."

I laughed lightly and shook my head. I knew that was coming. "We'll deal with that as needed. There's always online classes. It's like you're just going to class just to go. You have the credits you need to graduate."

She nodded. "That's true, but I still want to finish the classes. I guess online wouldn't be that bad to finish things off. I'll talk to my professors tomorrow."

I leaned down and kissed her juicy lips. "Cool. So you straight?"

"I'm good, baby. Thank you for being so concerned, but I'm good. I promise."

I didn't believe her, but I wouldn't keep pushing the subject right now. What my dad said kept ringing in my head, though. I wondered if the way she drank was linked to her father in any way. I couldn't just come out and ask, because I knew she wasn't going to be very receptive. I needed to know what we going on with her because I loved her, and I needed her to love me back one day soon. For that to happen, she had to let me in.

"Come on," I said, grabbing her hand. "Ma probably in tears right now. She thought she offended you."

"I'm going to make sure she knows she didn't."

"She good," I said, wrapping my arm around her shoulder. "Plus, I have a surprise for her and Pops that I know they will appreciate. For your mother as well, but she already knows."

"What surprise?" Nia asked suspiciously.

"You'll see."

Chapter 16

Keyton

I knew she was pissed off. She still wasn't leaving. Shit was too hot right now, and I didn't want her in the middle of this shit. I already was hiding too much. I felt bad because if she found out, I knew it would hurt her. I didn't want anything coming out until I was ready to explain.

"So," she yelled from the kitchen, "let me get this straight. You want me to be up under you twenty-four seven as if we ain't under each other enough," she said, coming out and flopping on the couch next to me. Her scent whooshed up to my face and mixed in with the Kush I was blowing. She always smelled good. "I have class! I'm grown as hell! I'm not doing that!"

I let the smoke from my blunt pass through my lips slowly, covering my face, before I blew it out. "Damn, Tori. Just for a few days until shit blow over. Then it's back to your regular scheduled program." I was agitated with trying to explain why I was asking this of her without giving her all the details.

She slid a hot wing into her mouth and took a bite. I looked at her sideways. "You didn't ask me if I wanted some wings, Tori."

She looked back at me. "You didn't ask me if I wanted to be stuck in the house like a three-year-old, either, but we ain't gon' start naming the things we didn't ask each other."

She smirked at me like that shit was funny. I swear, sometimes I wanted to just strangle her smart-mouth ass. I had something for her ass, though. "I'm out," I said, standing up.

She jumped up too. "Where the hell you going, Keyton?"

I looked down at her. "I got shit to handle."

She clasped her hands together in front of her and bit her bottom lip. She chuckled a little, and that was a clear indication that she was about to be on my ass. "You about to leave and I can't?"

She didn't realize how childish she sounded. I bent down to kiss her cheek. "I got shit to do, Tori."

"I got shit to do as well, Keyton," she mocked.

I had to laugh at her. "You so silly. I'm coming right back. I just need to make a run."

She crossed her arms over her chest. I took a moment to admire her. She had her hair in a high bun on her head, and she wore a loose-fitting Dallas Cowboys sweater and some black tights. Her feet were covered in some black fuzzy socks. She looked relaxed and sexy.

"I don't give a fuck, Key. I am not sitting in this big loft by myself all weekend. Especially if you about to leave!" She stormed off down the hall and slammed the bedroom door.

I ran my hand down my face and exhaled. This was my fault. I had her ass like this. She wanted to have everything her way, and the minute shit didn't go Tori's way it was hell on earth. I walked down the hallway and opened the bedroom door. She had her Coach overnight bag on the bed and was stuffing clothes into it.

"Where you think you going?" I asked, coming into the room and closing the door.

She didn't give me a second glance as she continued packing. "I'm going to Nia's."

I shook my head. "Nia ain't there. Neither is Mrs. Diane. Mon sent Mrs. Diane to the Bahamas for a week with Mrs. Porsha, Mr. Miles, and Winter's family. Nia is at Mon's. Winter is at Marco's.

She stopped packing and looked at me. She studied me, and I realized she was on to what was going on. "So, where are my parents?"

I knew she was getting the drift of how serious this shit was. "They are in the Bahamas for a week as well."

She walked up to me. "So what the hell is going on, Key? What are you not telling me?"

I licked my lips. I didn't want her stressed out behind this shit. I had everything under control. I just needed a little time to work out a few kinks. I saw the fear in her eyes as she looked at me. What I was about to say was going to fuck her up even more. "Someone has been following you. We also discovered that a similar van has been following Nia. It's been going on for weeks now."

She looked confused. "What?"

"We are handling it. I just need you to lie low for a minute."

"Wait," she said, shaking her head. "What the hell you mean following us? This shit ain't funny, Key."

"It's not a joke, Tori. I'm handling it."

"Why the fuck would anyone follow me?" She started pacing in front of me. She stopped and looked me up and down. "To get to you?"

I closed my eyes and sat on the edge of the bed. I didn't want to have this discussion right now, but it seemed I didn't have a choice. "Tori—"

"Why the hell would people come after you?"

"It's a long story."

She crossed her arms. "We got all night. Why would people be out to harm a business owner? What you got, the club and two restaurants? But that wouldn't make niggas want to kill you," she said, expressing herself with her hands. "What's going on?"

"It's a lot of shit, Tori. Things I can't explain to you right now. But in due time, baby."

She wasn't falling for my shit. She knew me better than anyone else in my life. I saw the moment the truth hit her, and it was a look I wasn't prepared for.

"You told me you stopped, Keyton. You lied to me!" she yelled.

I didn't have shit to say. I was stuck. Last year, we had a situation with a nigga and his crew from uptown. We set up a spot in his area and started taking his customers because our product was better. All that shit came down from Flacco. We were already making money, but the motherfucker couldn't leave well enough alone. To say the least, that started a war, which resulted in Tori being jumped by a few bitches from that side while she was leaving school. Also, she was three months pregnant with my seed. They almost killed her and were successful in killing our baby. That situation destroyed both of us. She left me as soon as she was physically able to do so and moved into her parents' place. She said she wouldn't come back until I was completely out of the game. I gave that shit all my effort because I didn't want to lose Tori. We had already lost our baby. I was out for about eight months, and then I found myself slowly getting pulled back in. Now, this shit felt like déjà vu. It seemed like every time a fuck boy had an issue with me, the first person they went after was Tori. They knew she was all I had, all that mattered.

My mom possibly lived somewhere with a rich nigga with her gold-digging ass. She never gave a fuck about me. As soon as she had me, she gave me over to the state. I didn't know any of my family. I was raised in the system and thrown out on my ass at eighteen. I tried to find her. My entire life became consumed with finding her. I knew if I did, then my life would be better.

Well, I did find her. Her name was Alice, and she didn't know who I was, and she wasn't concerned about me at all. I remembered spending a lot of nights crying to Tori about the way she treated me. It was as if she had no clue who I was, though I looked just like her. After fighting to find someone for so long only to have them deny you was possibly the worst thing a person could go through. I couldn't dwell on it, though. I had Tori, the love of my life, who was depending on me, so I had to do what I had to do. I had to give her all she ever wanted. I had been hustling since I graduated high school. I wanted to play college basketball, but the way my life was set up, that shit wasn't in the cards for me. I had to eat! To survive. I wanted the best for Tori.

Her parents were the perfect couple. Her father owned a construction company, one of the biggest ones in Dallas. He spoiled her, gave her everything she ever wanted. Her mother, Farah, was a stay-at-home mom and had been for about ten years. Before that, she was a teacher. They loved me to death. The last five years they took me in and treated me like I was their own, just on the principle that I was in love with their daughter. They had no clue about what I did outside of owning the club and the restaurants. My lifestyle wasn't flashy, so a lot of people looked at both Mon and me as if we were ordinary men, not drug kings. I kept my lifestyle as low-key as possible. Tori was used to a particular type of living. I did all I had to so that she could remain in that lifestyle, even with me.

"I can't believe this shit," she mumbled as she began pacing again. "How could I be so stupid? To think I mattered enough for you to actually change," she said in a low voice. I could hear hurt, pain, and disbelief. This lie was blowing up in my face.

"Baby, listen—"

"You said you opened the club so that you could clean your money. You and Mon sat and lied to my face!" Lemonte was going to catch it from Nia and Tori. Tori looked at him as a brother. He promised her he would stop at the same time I did. "What now? Watch my back everywhere I go? Watch for bitches with bats and brass knuckles?"

I looked up at her and shook my head. "If you just lie low while I handle it—"

I watched as tears formed in her eyes. "I can't keep going through this shit!"

I stood to grab her as she broke down. I couldn't promise to protect her, because in her eyes I'd failed in the past, but I would protect her with my life, against any niggas who got in the way. "I don't even know if this has anything to do with drugs, ma. Please, Tori."

"Let me go! All you ever do is lie to me, Key!" She cried harder as she pushed away from me. "After eight years, like, what the fuck?"

I wouldn't let her go. I couldn't.

"Then you want us to bring kids into this dys-functional shit? Our marriage is hanging on by a thread!"

I just held her tighter. I knew the reason we haven't tried to get pregnant again was because of the terrible time she had last time. She was so happy when she got pregnant, and so was I. We had been married and trying for years when it finally happened. They knew she was pregnant so they attacked her, resulting in her losing our first child. So all them niggas and the bitches who touched her had to die. I took care of that shit myself.

I held on to her until I felt the fight leave her body and she succumbed to the tears. I held her while she cried. Tried to be the comfort I thought she needed. I didn't want her heart to turn cold. I didn't want her to fall out of love with me. I mean, what's a man to do without his heart?

"I'm sorry, Tor."

Chapter 17

Tori

You would think after loving a man uncon-ditionally for so long that you would hold more value than to be lied to. I wanted so badly to just pack my things and leave, but truth be told, I had a hard time imagining life without Keyton. He was my best friend, the love of my life, my soul mate, my everything! The love I had for this man could not be put into words. Despite all the drama that so easily surrounded him, he was so easy to love. Beyond the physical attraction, I was still in love with him mentally. He was attentive and caring, and more than anything he cherished me.

These days, men like Keyton were hard to come by. I would be a silly woman to take the love and respect he constantly showed me for granted. I just couldn't believe I was right back in this position. Life on the line over some bullshit that didn't even pertain to me. I needed to come to the realization that I didn't matter to Keyton as much as he let on. I loved this man unconditionally through all the shit we'd been through. I gave my all to my marriage every step of the way. If he couldn't do the one thing I asked, then I couldn't say the same thing about him.

After two weeks of being in the house, I refused to live life like that. I couldn't continue to hide out waiting for Keyton to handle things. I needed to breathe! All I wanted to do was dance my ass off. I knew I couldn't do that at Pure without Keyton snatching me up. So I called Nia.

"Hello," she answered, sounding sleepy.

"Get up, bitch! We sneaking out!" I whispered as if someone were in the house with me.

I heard her shift around in Mon's bed. "Bitch, what?"

"You heard me," I said, laughing at myself. This was ridiculous. "We about to sneak out! I want to go to the club!"

"Why the hell we gotta sneak out? I am not trying to hear Mon's mouth. They told us to stay in!"

I rolled my eyes. "Bitch, you sound like you six! Get up, get dressed! I'm coming to get you!"

She smacked her lips. "You the one talking about sneaking out but I sound six?"

"Come on," I whined.

"Winter coming?" TaNia asked.

"Girl, Marco got her on extreme lockdown. She can't breathe in real deep without his permission."

TaNia laughed as I heard Mon walk into the room. "Baby, I got to make a run with Key and Marco. I'll be back."

"Really, Mon? So what am I supposed to do? It's Saturday night!"

"I know what day it is, Nia. Damn, just give me a few hours."

"You ask me to give you a few hours every day," Nia complained. "You leave me here to go do God knows what! I'm tired of this shit. I have work and school!"

"You ain't going back to that fucking job no way. Chill the fuck out wit'cho spoiled ass. I should have just dipped the fuck out without telling you shit!"

"Fuck you!" Nia spat.

Mon laughed at her. "When, shitttttt? Let me know," he laughed. "I'll be back, brat!"

I heard a door slam, and then Nia got back on the phone. "Fuck him! Fuck this! Give me twenty minutes!"

I was too ready. "I'll be outside in fifteen!"

***

TaNia and I decided to hit up Blue on the other side of town. Nia laughed beside me, which made me look over at her and smile. She was so goofy. Always happy, always laughing. I had been in the house too long. I needed to get out shake my ass and let my hair down.

As soon as the beat dropped, I started moving. I closed my eyes and threw my head back, letting the beginning of the song take me in.

"I can't wait to see you get your ass kicked," Nia said, still laughing as I started to move to "Let Me See the Booty" by The-Dream.

"If I'm getting my ass kicked, then so are you!" I said before I started dancing harder.

The club was turnt. I loved my husband with my life, and there was nothing that I wouldn't do for him, but I was tired. I wanted to be in love, be married, have children, and grow old with him, but that wasn't his dream. He wanted to run the streets, be a drug king, and have a lot of money. Since our dreams didn't match, I didn't see us being together forever anymore. It broke my heart to even think of life without Key, but my happiness and safety was mandatory.

I was in my zone dancing with Nia and sipping my drink without a care in the world. I knew we had been spotted by now and Key and Mon were probably on their way but what the hell. TaNia and I were just gon' turn up until we got shut down! I started to twerk my ass, standing up and looking back at it like it was going somewhere. I swung my hair from side to side and snapped my fingers.

"Work out, ho," Nia yelled over the music. She was showing out at this point too as we danced and laughed together.

We had the attention of every dude who didn't know better. Thankfully no one approached us. I was pissed at Keyton, but I didn't want to see anyone get caught in the crossfire. I literally had cabin fever. Don't get me wrong, I loved my loft, but being cooped up in it for two weeks was a bit much!

Initially, whatever needed to be handled would be done in a week. I was pissed about that, but I didn't trip because I could take a week, but two weeks? Hell no! I needed to interact with someone besides Key because I was two seconds from murking his ass. I loved Key something serious, but lately, with all these recent events, I couldn't help but think about the child he inadvertently caused me to lose. Sitting at home alone with my thoughts was the last thing he needed. The last thing I needed as well.

"Ohhhhhhh shit," I heard Nia say as she slowly stopped dancing.

"What?" I was about to turn around to see what she was looking at when this fine man stepped in front of me. "Oh, shit," I mumbled.

"Damn, baby, I feel like you dancing for me," he said, licking his lips. Now, I loved my husband. I really loved my husband. But, I had to give credit where it was due. This man's credit score was eight hundred. He had smooth dark skin covering his perfect body. He was tatted up. He wore a beach shirt with the sleeves cut off and some khaki shorts. He was tall, about the same height as Keyton. His lips were sexy, and he had sexy brown eyes.

"I'm just dancing," I found myself saying. "Not for anyone in particular."

I saw his homeboy, who was just as fine, approach Nia. Nia's eyes got big as she started to back away from him. I had to get us out of this shit.

"Look, I'm married," I said, thinking that would put an end to it all. "We were just leaving." I walked around him and grabbed Nia's hand. I didn't know what the dude was saying to her, but he had her smiling from ear to ear.

"That nigga let you go out, just you and your girl? By y'all damn self? As fine as y'all are?" He had a smile behind his eyes.

"Not really," I mumbled as I began to walk away.

"Don't leave, ma," he said, walking up to me and gently grabbing my arm. "I won't fuck with you." I didn't know what it was about him. I thought it was his finesse. He was smooth, the way he talked and the movements he made. The shit was alluring, and I was on the hook. "I'll just keep my ass in that corner," he said, pointing across the club.

"It's late," I said, looking everywhere but at him.

"You just got here," he said, smiling as I made eye contact with him. *How the hell he know when I got here?* "I saw you as soon as you walked in."

"I have to go," I said. Nia and I made our way through the crowd. Once we were outside, I breathed a sigh of relief.

"Them motherfuckers were fine," Nia said, laughing.

I laughed with her. "Girl, yes, they were!"

I looked down the sidewalk and saw two tall figures walking toward us at a fast pace. It would have scared the hell out of me if I didn't know who it was. I should probably still have been scared.

"Ay, pretty brown," I heard someone shout behind us. I looked back and saw that the fine dudes we were talking to had followed us out of the club. "I ain't catch your name!"

"Ohhh shit," Nia's drunk ass giggled.

"OMG," I whispered as Lemonte and Keyton continued to approach us. I looked at Nia. "Girl, on the count of three we gon' run our ass that way!" I nodded toward the other side of the street.

Nia was laughing hard as hell at my ass. She just wasn't aware how crazy Mon was. He never showed her that side, but I had seen his crazy too many times. Before we could take off, Key grabbed my arm and pushed me up against the building. I almost stumbled in my heels as he pushed me back. I could see he was pissed off.

"What the fuck I tell you, Tori?"

"Fuck you got on, Nia?" I heard Mon yell. "I told yo' ass I was coming right the fuck back! I should snatch yo' li'l ass up!"

I squeezed my eyes shut. I kind of felt bad. I mean, we weren't doing anything wrong, but I bucked the system. Now, I knew I would have hell to pay. "You are hurting me, Key."

"I don't give a fuck," he yelled. "You like to show your ass? That's what you like?"

I pushed him off me. Not that his big ass went anywhere. "I don't give a fuck, either! I can't sit in the house all day! I did that shit for two weeks, and we wanted to go out!"

"So, why you just didn't say that?" He was yelling in my face. "I would have taken you wherever you wanted to go!"

"Yeah, right, Keyton," I said sarcastically.

"Aye, pretty brown. You all right?" I heard the dude from the club yell. I closed my eyes because I knew Key was about to spazz.

"Say, playboy. Whether she all right ain't got a damn thing to do with you! I suggest you step yo' lame ass off!"

The dude's expression changed from concerned to pissed off really quick. "Who the fuck you talking to?" He started walking toward Keyton as if he wanted to fight, so Keyton released my hand.

He was still looking at me as the dude approached. He looked aggravated. Not at the dude. Not the fact that we were not on our side of town. He was still pissed about the fact that I left without him knowing. "You and Nia get y'all ass in the truck! Cortez parked right around that corner. Get the fuck in the truck and don't say shit!"

I didn't want to leave him out here to fight this dude over me, but at the same time, I didn't want to cause more drama by saying no. "Keyton, I'm sorry, okay? Let's just go!"

"Fuck that," he said, calmly stepping back from me. "Get in the car, Tori."

I saw Nia storm off in the direction that Key just pointed out, and I looked over to see Mon walking toward the dudes. I didn't want to see this go down, so I ran off behind her. Once we made it to the car, I was freaking out.

"I told him I was married! Why would he follow us?" I mumbled.

"Since Facebook made 'married' a relationship status as opposed to an actual commitment, people don't care no more." Nia sat on the opposite side of me, looking out the window.

"What did Mon say?"

She glanced over at me. "I couldn't even understand it all. I'm drunk off my ass, I got a headache, and my damn feet hurt! He was pisssssseeeddd! Talking 'bout, 'I'ma fuck you up! Keep playing with me! You don't fucking listen!'" she said, mocking him then laughing at herself.

I shook my head. "I'm sorry, Nia."

She frowned. "What you sorry for? We young, Tori. We did what they asked for two weeks. Putting ourselves behind in class. Not interacting with anyone while our parents vacation and our lives are put on hold."

"I know but—"

"You don't have to apologize to me," she slurred. "I had a good time."

The door on her side was snatched open. "Get your drunk ass out, TaNia."

She looked at Lemonte as the door to my side was opened and I was pushed over by Key. He got into the car and slammed the door. Looking at him, it didn't look as if he had a fight, but his breathing was an indication that he was still pissed.

"Call me, Tori," she said over her shoulder as she got out.

"Okay," I mumbled back as she got out of the truck. Silence fell in the confines of the car as we drove off.

I turned to Keyton. "Do you know where they going? Is she going to be okay?"

He didn't even look at me. He just kept gazing out the window until we got on the freeway headed downtown. I sat back in my seat and exhaled. "Did you fight? Is that guy okay?"

He looked over at me with a mug covering his handsome face. "Yo, you fucking that nigga?"

I was immediately offended. All the years I'd been with him, I had never once even entertained another man! "Fuck you, Keyton."

He laughed. "Yeah, fuck me!" He then turned in his seat toward me. "You didn't answer my question, Tori."

"I'm not answering that shit," I said under my breath.

Keyton got in my face. "Yes, the fuck you are!"

"Move," I said, looking in his eyes. "Get out my face!"

"What you concerned about him for?" He was still in my face, so I looked out the window.

"You can ask me that but can't tell me what's going on with Nia?"

He huffed. "TaNia good! She with Mon and you know that! What you not gon' do is avoid the real issue! Why the fuck was that nigga calling you and so concerned about my wife?"

"I don't know! Did you ask him were we fucking?"

He looked into my eyes for a minute. Both of us were just staring at each other. He smirked before he finally spoke. "Nah, I was too busy putting my Timbs in his mouth! So, if you were fucking that nigga—"

"I ain't fucking him! Tonight was my first time seeing him. He approached me, and I told him I was married!" I didn't know why I was emotional, but this was just too much. "I'm sooo tired," I said as I returned to gazing out the window.

"Tired of what?" Keyton yelled, startling me. "This life? Never having to lift a finger? Not having to work? Having a man who worships the ground you walk on and will do anything for you? Is that what the fuck you tired of, Tori?"

At that moment, we pulled up to the parking garage, and I jumped out of the truck with Keyton right behind me. He grabbed my arm roughly to stop me, and I snatched away from him.

"Is that what you tired of?" he yelled.

I kept walking, going into our building and up the elevator to our loft. I halted when I heard the door slam.

"Talk to me! What the fuck are you possibly tired of?"

I stopped walking. Maybe it was time I finally told Keyton what this lifestyle did to me and was continuing to do now.

I got in his face. "I'm tired of living in lofts and condos because you're scared that someone will try to burn down any house we get! I'm tired of not being able to have children with you because not only am I scared for their life, but I'm scared for ours! I'm tired of looking over my shoulder every day! I can't even halfway go to school because of you! I'm tired of this! I'm tired of us!" Tears ruined my makeup, but I didn't care. I needed him to hear me. "I'm tired of thinking of our child we lost when those bitches jumped me!" I saw his exterior soften as he looked at me. "That's what I'm tired of!"

I turned and continued into the bedroom. I threw random shit into a suitcase, and then I stormed back into the living room with it dangling in my arms.

Keyton stood when he saw me.

"Don't fucking touch me, Keyton," I cried as I walked to the door and then out of it.

Chapter 18

TaNia

The ride to Mon's loft was so quiet it made me nervous. He never drove in silence, so I knew something was wrong. I didn't understand why they were so upset. We went to the club to relax and have fun. That's what the average twenty-five-year-old does. I didn't see the issue.

When he pulled up, I was expecting him to do what he always did and open my door. But he didn't. He just got out of the car and walked up to the valet and handed him the keys. I was shocked, to say the least. I got out of the car and followed him slowly. When we got inside, he walked over to the linen closet.

"Wow. So, I get the silent treatment?"

He didn't respond as he grabbed a pillow and blanket from the closet and placed them on the couch.

"You didn't open my door. You didn't hold the door to the lobby open. So, what, when you pissed your manners leave?"

He threw the pillow and blanket on the couch then headed into the kitchen. I followed him. "So, you that mad?"

He looked at me for the longest time, just staring. He had a blank expression on his face. I didn't understand why he was tripping so heavy on me going out.

"I just went to the club, Mon."

He slammed the door of the refrigerator closed and turned to me. "You don't listen!"

I frowned and threw my hands up. "You don't talk!"

"Because I'm tired of talking! You need to start listening! If I ask something of you, it's for your safety! Right now, I don't want to talk to your immature ass."

He mean mugged me before he walked around me and back into the living room. I followed right behind him. He stopped abruptly, and I bumped into him. "Why the fuck you following me?"

"I'm trying to talk to you." I sounded drunk even to my own ears. I was trying my hardest not to laugh because he was so serious and I was so out of there. I held my head to the side and poked my bottom lip out. "I don't like you not talking."

I could see him trying not to smile. "Stop following me, Nia."

"Okay," I cooed. I placed my hands on my hips and exhaled, looking around his loft aimlessly, trying to find something else to do. I couldn't go home because my house was locked up. I couldn't talk to him because he didn't want to have anything to do with me. I knew calling Tori would be a dead end because she and Key were probably going at it in more ways than one. I folded my arms under my chest and exhaled deeply.

Mon looked over at me. "What? You just gon' stand there all night? Sit'cho drunk ass down somewhere!"

I wasn't dealing with his ass all night. I would get a room somewhere before I did. "Fuck this," I mumbled as I went to the table to grab my purse.

"Where the fuck you going?"

"Away from your ass," I yelled as I walked out the door and slammed it.

He was out the door after me. "You can't go nowhere without your car. I got your keys."

I stopped and looked in my purse, and sure enough, my keys weren't in there. "Shit," I mumbled as I made sure my wallet was there before

I zipped my purse back up. The heels on my feet started hurting. I couldn't walk far. "I should have changed my shoes." I walked back down the hall to him. "Give me my keys!"

He blew smoke in my face. "I ain't giving you shit. You can go back inside and sit down somewhere like I suggested."

I waved my hand in front of my face to push the smoke away. "Don't do that again."

He smirked as he took a long pull from the blunt and blew more smoke in my face.

"You so disrespectful!"

He shook his head, laughing. "Me? I'm the disrespectful one in the situation? Yo' ass couldn't even do the one thing I asked you to do. So yeah, I'm pissed off!"

I narrowed my eyes and shook my head. "Okay, so if you pissed off just say that! We are grown! You giving me the silent treatment and giving me attitude because you feel some type of way is for the birds."

We were in the hallway in front of his door. The spacing between the lofts provided a certain level of privacy. He stayed on the top floor, so basically, the only people who lived here were him and a young white couple. I gazed at him as he continued to smoke his blunt in my face.

I turned to walk away from him, and he grabbed me. "Chill out, TaNia! Damn!"

"No, you chill out, Lemonte!" I snatched away from him. "I asked you to stop, but you're childish and petty, so you keep doing the exact thing I asked you not to do!"

Lemonte laughed as he pulled me closer to him. "Childish and petty? That's how you feel?"

"Let me go, Lemonte," I spoke unconvincingly.

"Come back in the loft, ma. I'm sorry, TaNia. I just don't understand why you won't listen to me when I ask you to do something. You always on this super independent shit. Don't get me wrong, I love that about you, but sometimes I need you to just rock with me."

"I did exactly what you told me for two weeks. I wanted to get out, Lemonte!"

"Then say that, Nia. Say that to me! Fuck was gon' happen if some niggas from that side saw y'all and tried to do harm? I'd have to fuck this city up, TaNia."

I wanted so bad to blush, but I held it back. I loved when he said my name. The shit was so sexy. Everything about him was sexy. I knew where he was coming from, so I couldn't continue to fight him on something that I knew I was, to an extent, in the wrong for. "I'm sorry," I mumbled, looking down.

"Wait," he said, smiling. "What was that? Did you just apologize to the kid?" He released me and nodded. "Oh, shit! I think I may be getting to that ass."

"Shut up," I said, smiling.

He grabbed my hand and pulled me back toward the loft. "You love me, and I know it."

I shook my head no and twisted up my face, but deep down I knew I was lying. I'd been in love with him longer than I could remember, and honestly, I wasn't scared of loving him in secrecy. It kept me in a safe place. It kept my heart protected.

Once we were back inside, we went straight to his bedroom. "I wanna cuddle," he confessed as he pulled me to sit on the bed. He removed my heels.

"Oh wait," I said, teasing him. "Thugged-out Lemonte wanna cuddle and shit? Somebody record this!" I yelled as if someone else were in the room and could hear me.

He stood up, laughing. "Lay yo' crazy ass back," he said as he climbed on the bed with me. "Silly woman." He pulled me back to him and placed his face in the crook of my neck. He inhaled me as we drifted off to sleep.

I woke up with the worst headache in history. I squinted my eyes against the sun coming through the ceiling. I tried to sit up and had to lie back down, grumbling as I pulled the covers over my head. I heard footsteps coming up the stairs, and I knew it was Lemonte.

"I know you woke so take the cover off your head," he said as he snatched the covers.

"Please, baby," I said, pulling the cover back. "I want to sleep."

"You have been sleeping. We have to get up."

"What time is it?"

"One o'clock," he said, sitting on the bed. "Here, I made you breakfast, even though it's lunchtime."

I removed the covers and looked down at the tray he held in his hands. He made waffles, my favorite, and sausage, eggs, and French toast. My stomach growled as I grabbed the plate. "Thank you, Mon. I ain't gon' die eating this, am I?"

"Man, I swear," he said, laughing. "I been cooking since I was fo'!"

I laughed at him and shook my head as I grabbed the syrup and poured it on my waffles. He got up from the bed and walked over to the window to look out. "You not eating?" I asked with my mouth full.

He turned back around, and I had to admire him. The sun bounced off his skin, and his dreads were braided up. He smiled at me, and I felt as if

I would melt. "I already ate. I would like to talk to you about something once you're finished eating, if that's cool."

I nodded as I began to eat my eggs. It took me about fifteen minutes to finish eating because he was staring at me so intensely. I was nervous to talk to him, knowing it had to do with last night. Once I finished, he took the tray from me and took it downstairs. I was still sitting up on the bed when he returned.

I looked up at him. "I'm sorry about last night."

"Yeah," he said, sitting on the bed beside me. "What was that about?"

"Well, Tori and I wanted to get—"

He shook his head. "I'm not talking about that. We already discussed that, and it's over. I'm talking about the fact that you were drunk off your ass. In fact, you drink a lot, TaNia."

I shook my head and frowned. I mean, I drank, but a lot was a stretch. "Well, I'm grown as fuck for one."

"First, check your attitude." He looked at me with a very stern expression on his face. "That don't have shit to do with it and you know it."

I looked at him sideways. "Why you so upset?"

He shook his head and stood. "You didn't see you last night, TaNia. I did. You were all over the fucking place. I'm with the turn up and you know that, but last night was fucking embarrassing!"

I stood from the bed and got in his face. "Embarrassing? Really, Lemonte, I do apologize for embarrassing you, but if me doing what every adult does is embarrassing to you, then maybe we shouldn't be together."

"That's it right there, Nia. You hide and run from everything. Instead of dealing with it, you drown it in alcohol."

I was on the verge of tears because I never thought I would be called out. Especially by him. "I don't hide and bury anything! You make it sound like I'm always drunk."

"Most of the time you are. I didn't even know you drank like that. But my question is, why?"

"Why what?"

"Why are you always drunk?"

"I just said I'm not always drunk."

He reached his hand out to me, and I moved back.

"I'm an embarrassing drunk. I wouldn't want to be associated with no shit like that."

"Come on, TaNia. Talk to me."

I threw my braids over my shoulder. "What's this, Lemonte? An intervention or something?"

"Don't do that," he said, frowning. "Is it because of your dad?"

I laughed as I avoided the topic of my father. I hadn't gotten into a deep conversation about him since he passed, and I wasn't going to have one now. Just hearing his mother speak of him had destroyed me last time he was a topic, so I didn't plan on putting myself through that again. "I'm out."

He grabbed me and wrapped his arms around me and buried his face in my neck. "Don't shut me out, TaNia."

I shook my head and laughed. "Come on, Mon. You tripping."

"TaNia, talk to me, ma." His voice was low, but I heard him. I heard his love for me, his concern, and most of all I heard my friend. I couldn't talk. I didn't want to.

"Just let me go, Lemonte."

He spoke into my cheek. "I can't, TaNia. You have to face that fact that he's gone."

My entire body tensed. "I don't need you to tell me that! I know that!"

"But you haven't dealt with it."

I immediately became pissed off. "You don't know shit, Lemonte! Just let me go!"

He just held me tighter and kissed my cheek. "Please, TaNia. Talk about it."

I took a deep breath as I struggled against him. "Come on, Lemon—"

"I love you, TaNia. I see you hurting, and I want to help you heal, but you have to let me in."

I placed my head in my hands and screamed. I didn't want to face anything! I didn't want to hear anything. I didn't want to love him. I didn't want him to love me. I lost everyone I loved. I was tired of that shit. First it was my grandmother to breast cancer, then my grandpa to a heart attack, then my dad to prostate cancer. I didn't want to love. It was better to just not feel anything. To just drink.

"You can't love me, Lemonte," I cried softly.

"Why?" he asked. "I do love you, TaNia. Why you say I can't?"

"Because," I cried louder, "I lose everyone who loves me. Every-single-fucking-body! Please, don't love me."

I broke out in a deep cry that I been holding in for forever. I was expecting Lemonte to let me go and tell me to get out, but he didn't. He held me tighter. He constantly told me that he would never leave and that he loved me. I cried and screamed until my throat was sore and my voice was gone, and he just held me. I cried because I wanted to feel safe. I wanted to feel loved and needed. I wanted to let the fact that I wouldn't see my dad again settle into my heart. I cried for the woman I was now, but I had hope for the one I would one day be.

For the longest, I cried, and he just held me.

Chapter 19

Lemonte

I knew there was something with TaNia that wasn't right. She would open up to me to a point then shut all the way down. It seemed the only time she was completely free and open about anything else was when she drank. But after a crying spell that I felt would rip my heart out, she finally talked about her dad. She opened up to me about everything, and I listened because more than anything I wanted to be there for her. She finally told me that she loved me, had loved me since high school, and I was the happiest man on the planet.

I was headed to the office to check out the books and the new hire then headed right back to my baby. I was almost there when one of the baddest bitches I ever laid eyes on stepped in front of me. I mean, shorty was bad as fuck. "Shit," I let slip out before I could stop myself. I let my eyes move over her. She was about five feet seven inches, with a smooth caramel complexion and the sexiest fucking eyes. I couldn't place the color. It was a mix between maple syrup and hazel. She had thick, pouty lips and an oval face. She was built to perfection. Thick thighs, nice, round hips, and I hadn't seen it yet, but I would have bet a stack that ass was fat.

"Hello," she said, smiling at me.

I couldn't help but smile back. "You're kind of blocking the way."

"That's intentional," she said, moving directly in front of me. She was so close I had to take a step back.

"So you were intentionally slowing me down? I'm not sure I appreciate that," I said, looking at her.

"I'm sorry. I just wanted to introduce myself. I'm one of the new waitresses. My name is Delia Rose. They told me the boss would want to meet me."

TaNia gon' kill my ass. They ain't gon' ever find the body. "Whoever they were spoke correctly. You can step to the back into my office. The meeting will be brief. I just like to get a feel for the people who work for me."

"No problem," she said, smiling as she turned around.

Fuck my life! Her ass was the fattest thing on her. I grabbed my phone out of my pocket for a much-needed distraction. Once we were inside my office, I took a seat behind my desk as she sat across from me.

"Tell me about yourself," I said, still looking down at my phone. She was probably thinking I was rude as fuck, but I was trying to save both of our lives.

"Well," she spoke, "I attend UNT—"

My head snapped up. Was I being fucking set up? "You go to UNT?"

She smiled. "Everyone goes to UNT or TWU."

"I fucking see that," I whispered.

"Is that an issue?" she asked, frowning.

"No," I said, shaking my head. "Not at all. Um, what about family? Do you have any?" *Please be married!*

"Just me and my parents."

Fuckkk my life! "Did they discuss your shift with you?" She nodded, so I continued, "Any overtime needs to be run through me, so that would be a direct question. If for any reason you need to call out or leave early, run that through Val, the manager. Please don't make that a habit. I like consistency."

"I won't need any time off anytime soon," she replied.

"Things happen, Delia."

"I understand that, and if at any time I need time I will follow the procedure to call out. I just like consistency as well, you know?"

I nodded, and she giggled. Damn, was anything about this girl not sexy? "What's funny?"

She held up her hand. "I'm sorry, this is weird."

I frowned. "What's weird?"

"I never had a boss this young, and excuse me if I'm out of place, but attractive. I would like to think I could handle it."

I placed her file back on my desk and looked at her. "Handle it?"

"You know, deal with the fact that you're attractive. I mean, the other waitresses warned me, but I still wasn't prepared."

This was going to be a fucking issue. I leaned up in my chair and exhaled. "Look, I'm glad to have you aboard, but I keep a professional distance from all my workers. On top of all that, my baby is crazy as hell. I don't want you caught up like that, so my suggestion would be to keep it professional on your end as well."

She nodded, but I had a feeling she didn't plan on taking heed of my warning. "Scout's honor," she said, saluting me then giggling again.

I exhaled as she stood and walked her sexy ass out of my office. I looked down at my phone as it rang and TaNia's picture popped up. She was grinning big with her arms wrapped around my neck while I smiled harder. She must have done this shit. I didn't even like smiling.

"I see you changed your contact picture," I said, answering the phone.

"You better not change it, either," she warned.

"What yo' little ass gon' do if I change it, Nia?"

"Change it and see."

I laughed as I shook my head. "What's up, woman?"

"I'm hungry!"

"I'm at the restaurant if you want to come up here."

"Can you bring me a rib plate with some corn on the cob and mashed potatoes? Oh, and mac and cheese? Ask Mrs. Gordan to send me some cheesecake, too."

I frowned. "You want me to get all that and bring it to you? Why can't you just come up here?"

"That's too far," she whined.

"You just spoiled, TaNia."

"What the heck?" she said innocently. "First you don't want me to leave the loft, and now I'm spoiled because I'm asking you to bring me something to eat while I'm dying of starvation?"

I had to laugh. "You ain't dying, big head, but I got you. Can you give me an hour?"

She moaned into the phone. "I'll fall on my face by then."

I shook my head as I gathered my shit. "I'm on my way, TaNia."

"Yes! I love you."

"Yeah, whatever," I said, hanging up the phone. I laughed as I disconnected the call, and a knock sounded at my door.

"Come in." I didn't look up to see who the person was, but the scent was familiar. She had just left.

"I'm sorry," she cooed. "I have another question for you."

I leaned back in my seat and looked at her. "Yes, Delia."

"You own a strip club, right?"

I was confused by her question. "I do."

"Club Pure, like the hottest spot in Dallas. I've been a few times."

I looked at her sideways. "I'm only part owner, but yeah, it's one of my spots."

She stood across from me, looking at me for a moment. Neither of us spoke. She was just staring at me, licking her lips. "So, could I get hired there as well?"

"What?" I asked, thrown off by her question.

"Do I fit the requirements to strip at your club?"

I rubbed my chin as I sat back. "You would have to audition and find out, but if you don't mind, I have some shit to handle."

She smiled as she turned to walk out.

She could strip on the fucking moon and niggas would pay to see that shit! "I'ma have to cancel that bitch."

Chapter 20

Winter

I jumped up and down on Demarco's bed while he looked at me as if he wanted to kill me. "Because you're freakishly tall, your bed is freakishly big, and it makes me want to be a kid again! I love it."

"Get'cho overgrown ass down, girl," he said as he slid his jacket on.

I was out of breath, but I refused to stop jumping. "Come get me down," I challenged.

He looked up from buttoning his shirt and glared at me. "If you wanna go eat, you better get'cho ass down, Winter."

My jumping slowed as I looked at him. "You gon' mess with my food, though," I said, looking at him sideways. "That's not cool."

He laughed as he grabbed his watch and put it on. "That's why yo' ass fat, Winter. All you do is eat."

My mouth dropped open as I looked at him. "Did you just call me fat?"

"I didn't say that you were fat, Winter."

"That's what you basically just said."

"You not fat, woman. Can we go eat? I'm hungry as fuck."

I jumped down off his bed and pulled my dress back into place. I grabbed my black suede red bottoms and slid them on my feet. "Old man," I mumbled as I grabbed my clutch.

"My dick big, though," he mumbled back as we walked out the door.

I laughed at him as he held the passenger door of his Audi open so that I could get in. "I swear you get on my nerves," I said as I slid into my seat.

This was my reward. I heard about Nia and Tori sneaking out and going to the club. Demarco quickly and firmly warned me not to try that shit. So for the last two weeks, I'd literally been stuck in his house with him. But in that time, I'd learned so much about him. He told me about the time that he was homeless and living in shelters. He also told me about the man he met who pulled him from the Marines to make him a sniper for the Cartel, Lou. I cringed while he spoke about his time in the Marines and how, after that, he was a heartless person who didn't place value on anyone's life. He did the assignment placed in front of him with no regard for the person's life. It was hard to think of the man I was in love with in that manner, but that was his past, just like stripping was mine. We both agreed to never judge each other.

So, for good behavior, I was being taken to dinner at the Five Sixty by Wolfgang Puck in downtown Dallas at the top of the Reunion Tower. Demarco dressed in an all-black shirt and slacks with a burgundy suede jacket. His gold Rolex watch shined as he turned the wheel of his all-white Audi to get on the highway.

When we made it, he opened my door and gave the car key to the valet. I smiled at him as we walked inside.

"Reservations for Winter," he said to the host.

The host smiled as he grabbed menus. "Right on time," he said, smiling at me. "Follow me to the elevator."

We walked to the elevator that had a backdrop of downtown Dallas. I was low-key scared as hell, so I made sure not to look down. Demarco walked in and placed his back against the glass, pulling me into him. I intentionally pressed my ass into him as he kissed my neck. "This is so nice, Demarco," I said, smiling as I leaned my head to the side to give him even more access to my hotspot. He immediately kissed me there.

"I'm gon' be a real gentleman," he mumbled. "I'm opening doors and pulling chairs out," he said as he grabbed my ass. "I'm tryin'a get my dick wet."

I rolled my eyes and tried to move away from him. Sometimes he said the most unemotional shit to me. I felt like a live-in sex slave. "That's sweet," I said sarcastically.

"Why you moving?" he asked against my neck.

"I hate the way you talk to me sometimes," I stated in a low voice.

"What I do?" he said innocently. "I dressed up, I opened your door, I'm attentive," he said, squeezing me. "I deserve some, Winter. I've been a good boy."

I smiled as he kissed me. He looked good, he smelled good, and what he said was true. He had been nothing but attentive. I loved Demarco so much, and though he hadn't said it yet, I knew he loved me as well. "I love you."

He turned me around to face him and kissed my lips. "You like the only thing that matter to me, Winter. Before you came, I didn't have much of anything to keep me going. You make living purposeful. You know that, right?" he said, kissing me again. "You should always know that, baby."

"I know."

"Here we are," the host said as we stepped off the elevator, leading us to our table in the middle of the restaurant.

We sat down and quickly ordered our food. This was by far one of the nicest restaurants in Dallas, and I was so glad he picked it. The food was good, and the atmosphere was sexy.

"This is so good," I said as I grabbed my wine.

"I'm glad you enjoying this high-ass food," he said, looking down at his sushi roll.

"Really, Demarco," I said, annoyed.

"All right," he said, smiling up at me. "I'm sorry, ma'am. I won't complain about the prices and shit."

"Please. You the cheapest person I know, Demarco."

"So?" he said, shrugging his broad shoulders. "That's how you keep money: think big and act broke."

"Whatever, boy, you just cheap period."

He laughed as he sipped his drink. He leaned back in his seat and just looked at me. "What else would you like to do after this?"

I sipped my wine, looking at him over the glass before I set it back down on the table. "What did you have in mind?"

"I didn't plan anything past this. We can take one of those horse carriage rides. Is that romantic enough?"

I rolled my eyes and shook my head. "You shouldn't want to be romantic enough, Demarco. You should want to be romantic at all times. I cook for you, I massage you, I cater to your every need."

"But I don't ask you to do that shit, Winter. I'm not complaining, but I never asked you."

"That's the point. You don't have to ask me. I do it because I love you." I watched as his large frame shifted in his seat. "Me telling you that I love you shouldn't make you uncomfortable, Demarco."

"It doesn't make me uncomfortable, Winter. Damn, can we not do this right now? I would rather enjoy the night."

I scraped my fork against my plate before setting it down. "You right. I'm sorry."

He looked past me at a table behind me where a couple was sitting, completely engrossed in each other. I moved my head to the side to break his eye contact, and he looked at me. "What?"

"I said sorry," I said, annoyed.

"Apology accepted," he mumbled, looking to the side of us.

"Demarco, are you even paying attention to me?"

He grabbed his phone and sent a quick text before he looked back at me. "I am, Winter."

"Are you sure? Because I don't feel like you are."

"I'm sorry," he said, looking at the table across from us again. Two men looked to be having a business meeting.

"Why are you looking at people?"

He grabbed his phone when he got a text back, and the look on his face turned completely cold. I leaned back in my seat and began looking around as well. The air around us stilled to a crisp as he leaned forward in his chair. "Demarco," I mumbled nervously.

"Go to the restroom, Winter. Go to the very last stall, lock it, and stay there until I come to get you."

"Demarco, please tell me what's going on," I pleaded with him.

"It's complicated. I just need you to listen to me, baby. I'll be there to get you in a minute."

"But what if you don't come?" I whispered.

"You owe me some, Winter," he said, giving me a sneaky grin. "I'm fucking coming."

I exhaled deeply as I stood. He stood with me and buttoned his jacket. I went to walk past him, but he gently grabbed me and pulled me to him. "You're all that matters, Winter," he said as he kissed my cheek. "Give me five minutes."

Chapter 21

Demarco

I couldn't believe I didn't see this shit when I walked in. A fucking setup. I watched Winter as she nervously walked to the restroom. I just prayed that no one was in there. I sat back down slowly as I pulled my Desert Eagle from my back, unnoticed to them as I placed a silencer on it. I didn't know how many enemies I had to take out, but I knew I was coming up out of this motherfucker.

I thought putting the reservation in Winter's name would be discreet enough, but I guessed whoever was after us had her information as well. I watched the woman who was so engrossed in her "date" stand after seeing Winter walk into the restroom. She kissed the man on the cheek and began walking to the restroom. Before she could make it past my table, I stood and grabbed her, placing the gun to her head.

The civilians ran, and the motherfuckers sent to kill me had their guns pointed at me. I quickly counted six semiautomatics.

I looked down at the bitch in my arms, noticing that she was as clearly shaken. "Who sent you?" I said in a low voice.

"Fuck you," she spat in a Russian accent.

"Nah, I'm gon' pass," I replied nonchalantly as I pressed my gun to her temple. "I don't have time to fucking play with y'all," I said to the others. "So, we either about to tear this motherfucker up or y'all gon' let me and my girl walk out this bitch. Y'all choice, but you only got ten seconds."

They started yelling shit to each other in Russian as I started counting to ten. When I got to ten, I pushed the woman away from me and started shooting. I saw the woman get shot in the head and drop to the ground before I made it to the corner. Glass flew and chairs broke into pieces as I watched gun smoke fill the air. I let them let off as much as their hearts desired. I heard screaming coming from the restroom, and I knew it was Winter. I looked past the wall and saw one of the shooters walking over to see if I was dead. As soon as he got close enough, I put my gun to his head and dropped him, only causing more gunfire to erupt.

"These motherfuckers want my head," I said as I placed my Desert Eagle on my back. I grabbed the semiautomatic of the dead motherfucker closest to me and start busting. Before I knew it, seven bodies were on the ground and the restaurant was fucked up.

I quickly busted into the bathroom and into the last stall. Winter screamed again when the door banged against the wall. "Oh, my God," she said, grabbing her chest.

"Are you all right?" I asked, breathing hard.

"What the fuck was that?" she asked, clearly shaken up.

"Come on, I'll explain later. We have to get the fuck out of here," I said as she reached out to grab my hand.

I covered her face as we walked by the bodies on the floor then went down on the elevator. There was a commotion in the lobby, so I kept my head down and got to the car as fast as I could.

When we made it back to the house, I immediately called Mon and Key. "Man, I just had a fucking shootout at the restaurant with Winter." I spoke fast as I paced my living room. Winter had retreated to the bedroom somewhere. She wouldn't even look at me let alone speak to me.

"What the fuck you mean a shootout?" Key yelled.

"Seven Russians," I said, still pacing. "They were sent to kill me, but they wouldn't tell me who sent them. Winter fucked over, man. She won't even talk to me."

"But y'all all right? Y'all good?" Mon asked.

"Physically she good, but mentally I can tell she fucked over, man. Fuck," I yelled in frustration.

"What about you, Marco?" Key asked.

"I'm fucking good," I said, tugging my jacket off. "I'm fucking good," I repeated as I looked down at my hands, which were shaking like they did every time I caught a body. I hadn't had to kill anyone in years, so I couldn't wrap my head around the shit. My heart rate hadn't slowed down, and I felt sweat forming on my brow. *Fuck!* I didn't need to have an anxiety attack right now. I had to check on Winter.

"Marco," I heard Key yell through the phone. "What you want us to do?"

I took deep breaths and closed my eyes. "Just lie low. Do whatever you were doing before. It's all good, man."

"You sound crazy, Marco," Mon said. "You just caught a bunch of bodies. The cops could be on the way to your spot. There is no fucking way someone didn't see you."

"Mon, I can't think about that shit right now. Key, call Detective Smith and tell him what the fuck happened. I'll call Lou."

"Lou?" Marco asked suspiciously.

"Yeah," I said, sitting down for a second before standing back up. "I'll call Lou."

"You don't think it's too soon for that shit, Marco? I mean, we don't even know who behind this shit."

"We have been trying to figure that out for months, Key. You got any other fucking ideas?"

"Hold off on that phone call, Marco. The fewer heads we have in this shit, the better. You just check on Winter, make sure she's straight, and I'll call Detective Smith. If we need to involve Lou, we'll call him later. Mon, ain't you at dinner with TaNia?"

"We were just leaving. We got a room downtown for tonight."

"Be safe," I said. "This shit getting crazier, and we still don't really know shit!"

"I got Cortez with me. You with Tori, right?"

"Nah," he said in a low voice. "She been at her parents' all week, but I got a detail on the house. I'm going to get her tomorrow."

At that moment, I saw Winter walk into the living room. "I gotta go! Say, call me when you get settled tomorrow so we can link up. Graduation is next week. We need to get our shit together."

"Bet," they both said as they disconnected the call.

I looked at Winter for a minute, not knowing what to say. She looked at me with those soul-searching eyes, and I literally felt my anxiety vanish.

"Are you okay?" she asked.

"Are you?"

She nodded, and I wanted to believe her, but I knew better. "Winter, I—"

"I just want you to be good! If you're good, then we can talk about it." She walked deeper into the living room.

"I'm good."

She nodded. "So let's talk."

Chapter 22

TaNia

I sat in the truck so nervous I could scream. I wanted to tell Cortez to pull off and take me somewhere far as hell, but all that shit talking I just did got me into this position. I was going to learn to shut my mouth one day.

I heard Cortez's phone ring through the partition that separated us. He then opened his door to get out and open mines. "Ms. Nia, Lemonte advised me to walk you up." He reached in to offer his hand, and I accepted.

The walk to the room had my palms sweating. Cortez was awkwardly quiet. He didn't talk much at all, but he could say something. I looked up at him. "So, um, ready for football season?"

He smirked over at me as he pushed the button to call the elevator. "I am."

I nodded. "What . . ." I stammered. "Who team do you like?" I said, sounding slow.

He laughed at that. I thought he knew what Lemonte had planned, and he had a good idea about why I was freaking out. We stepped into the elevator, and he pressed the button for the top floor. "I'm a Broncos fan."

I scrunched up my face. "That's the green team, right? With the, umm, the eagles?"

He shook his head. "No, that's the Eagles."

I laughed uncomfortably. "Right," I said, scratching my head. "That makes sense."

The elevator came to a stop, and the doors swooshed open dramatically. Cortez stuck his hand out the doors. "To the right, at the end of the hall."

I slowly stepped off the elevator and turned in the direction in which he pointed. "You not coming?"

Cortez laughed loudly. "Umm, you want me killed? Hell no, I'm not coming. I wouldn't keep the man waiting, Nia." He pressed the button to close the elevator doors. "Room 2000."

"That's such a weird number," I mumbled as I started down the hallway. It felt like the green mile. I looked behind me at least twenty times. My hair began to stick to my neck and upper back. My dress felt tighter, and these heels were killing me. When I got within ten feet of the door, my heart started pounding. "I can't do this!"

I turned around to go back to the elevator when the room door opened. "Where you going, baby?"

I turned around to face Lemonte. He had removed his blazer and now only wore his slacks and a muscle shirt. His dreads were now braided back into two thick ones. The brown tips contrasted with his light brown eyes. He looked good enough to eat.

"I left something in the car." It sounded like a lie when I said it.

He smirked because he knew I was lying. "What you leave?"

"My cell phone. I told Tori I would call to, umm, see if she—"

I looked down at my clutch as my phone rang inside it. I looked up at him and saw his phone pressed to his ear. I just smiled as I let it ring. I was busted. This nigga left a voicemail.

"Umm hello, Nia's phone. Can you please tell your very beautiful owner to get her thick ass in this room? Oh, and yo' ass better not interrupt this shit that's about to go down! You hear me?" He licked his lips and bit into his bottom lip as he turned his phone off and slid it back into his pocket.

If his ass weren't so sexy! I laughed as I grabbed my phone out of my purse and turned it off.

"Anything else?" he asked as he leaned against the doorframe.

I shook my head as I began to walk into the room. I could hear soft music, but I couldn't make out what it was. As soon as I crossed the threshold, the opening to "If You" by Silk begin to play. That was my shit! Mon closed the door and placed a glass of champagne in my hand as I continued to walk past him. Everything seemed to go in slow motion. The decorations inside the room were beautiful. Roses covered the floor and bed. A tray of chocolate-covered fruit sat beside it. He had the curtain slightly open, so the moon peeked through. Outside of that and the candlelight, the room was dark. I heard him move behind me and I flinched. Taking a deep breath, I downed the champagne.

"You nervous?" His voice was deeper than usual and low. Sexy as hell!

"Umm, a little!"

He chuckled as he walked around to face me, still hovering over me though I had heels on. "Why? I'm going to take care of you, Nia. I promise."

I nodded slowly. I couldn't back out. He had been patient and understanding, and this was the man I was in love with! Had been secretly since high school. I wanted him. I needed him to make me a woman.

He stepped closer to me and ran his hand down my arm. We both watched the movement. He then stuck his tongue out to run it across my bottom lip slowly before sliding his tongue inside my mouth.

I could taste the vodka he drank earlier as it mixed with the champagne I just indulged in as well as his natural taste. I felt the need to hold on to something, so I wrapped my arms around his neck. He started kissing my neck and backed me up to the bed.

He broke off the kiss to look into my eyes. Nothing but lust and admiration sang in their dark depths. "Sit down."

I did as I was told as he reached down to remove my heels one at a time. He then climbed on top of me so that I had no choice but to lie down. I heard the song change. Twista's "Wetter" was now playing.

I closed my eyes as his hands caressed my thighs. I was apprehensive about him seeing me completely naked, but it was too late to turn back now. He kissed my thighs as he moved my dress up my body. He trailed kisses over my stomach and arms as I sat up for him to take the dress off. I searched his eyes to see if his expression would change. It didn't. I still saw lust and admiration as he licked his lips, looking down at me.

"Lemonte?" I whispered.

He smiled down at me. "Yes, ma'am?"

"And my body?"

He returned his gaze to my body as he reached down to slowly remove my panties. He smiled, possibly recalling the first time I asked him that question. "What about this muthafucka?"

I bit my lip as he removed my bra. "It's not too much?"

He leaned down to kiss me, sliding his tongue into my mouth and fucking up my thought process. "It's perfect," he whispered.

I moaned as his fingers slid between my folds as he looked into my eyes. "Damn, TaNia, you wet already? That's how you feel."

I closed my eyes as his finger moved over my clit slowly, causing my body to jerk with every stroke. "Damn," I moaned out.

"Open your eyes, Nia. I want you to see me!"

Our eyes locked as he slid his fingers inside me, then brought those same fingers up and placed them inside his mouth, sucking me off his fingers. "You taste good," he cooed before he shifted on top of me to remove his shirt. I licked my lips and looked up at him, smiling. He was so beautiful. Everything about him turned me on.

He trailed kisses from my breasts, licking and sucking them as his finger returned to my pussy.

He grabbed a strawberry from the tray beside the bed and placed it into my mouth. He bit the opposite end, causing the juices to slide out of my mouth. He licked the corners of my mouth, moving all the way down to my breasts before he placed a kiss at my entrance.

I gasped as he pulled me down and pushed my legs back. "There go my girl! I been dying to meet you," he spoke as his tongue slid between my folds. My legs came down naturally.

"Pull them muthafuckas back, Nia. I gotta talk to shorty real quick." He smiled as his face disappeared between my legs.

"Ohhh fuck!" I cried out every time his tongue slid over my sensitive clit. "That feels so good, baby," I announced as he slid his finger inside me. My body jerked with every motion, little involuntary spasms, as his tongue matched the movements of his finger inside me. I felt my orgasm sneak up my spine, and I screamed out, drowning out the music and the slurping sounds he was making. My entire body quaked as I gripped the sheets covering the bed. I cried out his name as he continued to feast on me until my shakes subsided. I closed my eyes, allowing whatever awaited me to run freely. I heard him protect himself before he got back into the bed with me.

He grabbed my legs as he moved to my center. "Put me inside you."

I reached down and placed the head of him at my entrance. Our eyes connected, and I knew at that moment that I was giving myself to the right man. I could feel the love that he had for me in every glance, touch, and kiss. I wanted him to be the first and only man to experience me on such an intimate level. "I love you," I moaned as he began to enter me. "Just go slow, baby. Please don't hurt me."

"I would never hurt you, TaNia."

He buried his face in my neck as he made the first attempt at entering me. I squeezed my eyes shut as he continued to move forward. My fingers dug into his biceps as I bit into my bottom lip to suppress the scream that threatened to escape. He and I both gasped at the same time as he moved back out of me then entered again.

"I love you more, baby," he moaned. "You belong to me, TaNia Monae."

"Yes," I replied. I wasn't even sure if that was a question. Pleasure replaced pain in a matter of minutes. I guessed he could tell, because he pushed my legs back farther, going deeper. I felt him in the pit of my stomach.

He shifted again and went deeper, and my legs went numb. The grip I had on the cover slipped as my eyes rolled. "Ohhh fuck! Don't stop, Mon! Please don't stop!"

"Right there? That's it?" he groaned as he drilled into me slightly harder than before.

"Yesssssss, shit! That's it," I cried out. "That's it," I whimpered weakly.

My body gave out as he slammed into me. I was defenseless as he continued to hit my spot! My entire body immediately responded to how deep he was.

"That shit feels so good. Cum on that dick, baby!" He pulled out of me and flipped me over, pushing my ass in the air. "Don't move," he warned as he entered me from the back.

His strokes were long and measured, purposely placed to drive me insane, and I couldn't do nothing but take it. He sped up, catching me off guard as he slammed into me. "Lemonte!"

His hand came down on my ass, making the sound echo across the room.

My heart raced, mind gone. All I wanted to do at this point was throw the towel in. "I can't take it," I confessed loudly.

"It's yours, baby," he said back. "Handle that muthafucka!"

I gripped the pillow in front of me as he grabbed my waist and moved deeper. Faster. My toes curled as another orgasm took over me. I tried to get away from his grasp, but he held me down, sliding into my pussy faster and making my orgasm ten times more intense.

"I told yo' ass not to move," he groaned as he pinned me down.

I squeezed my eyes shut, wishing to find some relief, but there was none. He ran his hands through my hair then down my back before he smacked my ass again. He then placed both his hands on my back and began deeply stroking me. "Ohhhhhh fuck! Monnn!"

"You feel that shit?" he asked, smacking my ass again. "Come for me, Nia."

"Yeah," I cried out. "I'm coming!"

I placed my hand on his stomach to stop him from going deeper, and he slapped it away. "Move that shit, Nia. Take this dick!"

"Oh fuckkkk!"

"Shit," he grunted. "TaNia!"

As another orgasm racked my body, I could only process two things. One was that after all these years of secretly wanting Lemonte, I had him. The second thing was I was no longer a virgin.

Chapter 23

Keyton

I had to get to Mon and Marco to get all the details of the shit that popped off at the restaurant, but I needed to talk to Tori first. We argued. I yelled. She screamed. That shit went down all the time, but something about last time was different. I saw something inside Tori that I'd never seen before. She had pure hatred in her eyes. I tried leveling with the situation. Like maybe I was reading too deep into some shit, but my heart told me what I saw was exactly what she felt.

I jumped out of my Bentley and nodded at the security detail I had stationed outside her parents' house. I walked up the steps to her parents' crib. I called earlier, and her pops confirmed that she was here. I needed to see her. I needed to know that all hope wasn't lost for us. If Tori left me, then I felt sorry for any nigga who rubbed me the wrong way. Tori had successfully suppressed the beast inside me. Without her, shit was going to get crazy.

I rang the doorbell a few times before her mother opened the door. "Hey, Ma," I spoke as I leaned down to kiss her cheek. She hugged me back and kissed my cheek. It was crazy. The woman in front of me loved me more than the one who gave birth to me. I was just her son-in-law, but an outsider looking in would think she pushed me out herself.

"Hey, baby! I missed you," she said, still holding me. I kissed her cheek again then stood straight.

"I missed you too. Did you enjoy the Bahamas though?"

She smiled. "We had a great time. Thank you so much for sending us! We needed it. Lately, Ray has been stressed with a lot of things, and we needed the getaway."

I frowned. "What's stressful about construction?"

Momma Farah, as I called her, looked up at me and smiled weakly. "He has a lot on his plate, Keyton. I've tried telling him to slow down before he gives himself a heart attack, but he doesn't listen to me when it comes to work. I just wish he would, Keyton. I'm scared of what will happen if he doesn't."

The look of pain on her face tugged at my heart. Watching the marriage between Tori's parents gave me a good idea of how to handle my own. Besides the fact that they were hopelessly in love with each other, they also respected each other. You could tell that even after thirty years of marriage, they still loved each other. I craved that. I needed it. I had to have it with Tori.

I placed my hand on her shoulder. "It'll work out, Momma. Don't worry. He is built to last a long time."

She smiled. "I didn't mean to hem you up in the door with my personal problems. Come on in." She stepped aside for me to enter. I automatically looked up the staircase because I knew that was where Tori was hiding out.

"I'm sure you're here to obtain your wife. She's upstairs moping around. She hasn't come down to eat or anything. I try to mind my own business, but it seems like you two are in a rough place."

I looked back at Momma Farah and nodded. "We are," I admitted. I exhaled deeply as I ran my hand down my face. "I think Tori still blames me for what happened to her. She tells me that she doesn't trust me. She thinks everything that comes out of my mouth is a lie. She'll believe anyone over me. I can't get it right."

"Tori knows what those people did to her wasn't your fault," Momma Farah said, looking up at me. She grabbed my hand in hers. It was funny because she had to grab one of my hands with two of hers. She was a little lady. "Hang in there with my baby, Key. You love her. She knows that, and she loves you back. Just be patient with her, son."

I nodded and adjusted my hat with my free hand. "I'm not giving up on us."

Mrs. Farah smiled. "That's what I like to hear. G'on on up there."

I leaned down and kissed her again before I took the stairs two at a time until I came to Tori's room door. I could hear "Not Gon' Cry" by Mary J. Blige being played softly and Tori singing horribly over it. I laughed and shook my head. My baby was so dramatic. I opened the door and actually laughed out loud at what I saw. Tori had her hair brush in her hand with her head thrown back, trying her hardest to keep up with MJB. She didn't even notice I was in the room.

"Yoooooo, you killing all the cats and dogs on this side of Dallas!"

Tori jumped back and looked at me. I could have sworn I saw her smile a little before she reached over and turn her Beats Pill off. She placed the brush on the dresser and walked over to me. "What are you doing here, Keyton? I thought I told you I didn't want to see you."

"I ain't give a fuck," I said nonchalantly as I lay across her bed. She could miss me with this attitude. I wasn't feeling it.

"Well, that's nothing new." She stood a few feet away from the bed with her arms crossed and a frown covering her beautiful face. She wore a white T-shirt with black tights. I could see her nude bra through her shirt. I wanted so bad to touch her, but I couldn't risk her shooting my ass.

I leaned up on my elbows to look at her. She had this cute-ass pout while bouncing her leg like she was ready to pounce on my ass. We were prepared to fuck each other up in two very different ways. "You done with this temper tantrum? You ready to come home?"

She crossed her arms over her chest. "I told you I'm not coming home. I'm getting my own place, and I start work next week."

I stood from the bed and got in her face. "Fuck you mean you getting your own place? You need to dead that shit! You have a home with me."

"No, you have a place," she said, jabbing her finger into my chest.

"We fucking married! Ain't no me and you! It's just us! Ours! We! We have two places. The loft and the condo! You want a house? Cool, I'm getting one built from the ground up. You still want to work? Cool, you'll work for me! You want a daughter? Take your clothes off."

Tori looked at me like I was crazy, but I meant that shit. She wasn't thinking straight, so I started making moves to prove to her that I wasn't lying when I said it was all about her. I meant that from the bottom of my heart. I wanted to be with Tori, and if giving her all the things she wanted from me, including my time, would make that happen, then so be it.

"You think coming in here and saying all that will magically make me come back? I need proof. I need to know you changed. I need to know I can trust you, Keyton."

I pulled out the blueprints to the house from my back pocket and placed them in her hand. I then pulled her job offer to be the manager of my three restaurants from my other pocket and put it into her other hand. "I didn't bring any condoms."

She looked down at the blueprints and the letter and frowned. "What is this?"

"That's me giving you what you want, Tori. This is me being your husband. I don't give a fuck what these other hoes talking about. You all I want and see!"

"You just want to be in control, Keyton. You want me to fold, but that's not going to happen easily. I'm done with all the bullshit that comes with you! Comes with this marriage."

"That's bullshit and you know it! I ain't tryin'a hear that shit, Tori. So get your shit so we can go!"

"Can you fucking hear?" She was yelling in my face as if that shit was supposed to scare me off or some shit. "I'm not leaving!"

"So, I'm moving in here?" I asked as if what she said didn't matter. "A'ight, cool. Let me go get some shit from the house and I'll be back."

I turned to leave the room, and she ran in front of me, blocking me from leaving. "What the fuck, Key?"

"Fuck is you blocking the door for?"

"You can't move in here. Are you crazy?"

I shrugged. "I have been called a lot of shit!"

She pushed me farther into the room. "You don't run shit!"

I hardly moved. Her little ass wasn't gon' do shit. "Yes, the fuck I do. I spent a month giving you the space you fucking asked for, but that shit over now. Get'cha shit so we can go!"

She ran both hands through her hair and exhaled deeply. I knew she was pissed off, but apparently, I didn't give a fuck! I was over all this shit. She was either coming willingly, or I was bringing my shit right up in here.

She looked at me as she weighed her options. "Keyton, this shit is unnecessary!"

"You're my wife, so I see this shit as mandatory," I said as I smiled at her.

"Don't fucking smile at me! I ain't playing with you, Keyton. I'll punch you dead in yo' shit! That's how pissed off I am!"

"Be pissed off!" I licked my lips as my smile deepened. "Bust me in my shit, and I'ma fuck you up against that wall. You don't want ya momma hearing who you really call daddy, do you?"

She shook her head as she went to grab her phone and purse. "I can't fucking stand you!"

"Yeah. Yeah, I know, I know. Now get'cha shit," I said as I grabbed her phone from her hand. Before I could stop her, she reached up and slapped my ass. I grabbed her by her arms and pushed her back onto the bed and got on top of her. "What I tell you about your fucking hands, Tor?" I spoke as I settled between her legs. She thought I was playing with her ass.

"Get the fuck off me," she said, looking into my eyes.

"Fuck no," I said, kissing her on the lips.

"Move, Keyyyy!"

"I ain't moving shit! I just told you what would happen if you put your hands on me," I said, moving to kiss her neck. I wanted to touch her, but I didn't trust her not to keep her hands to herself. I continued to place kisses all over her face and neck. I took my tongue and slid it across the top of her breast before I bit her nipple through her shirt.

I heard her moan. She could try to hide it all she wanted, but I knew her pussy missed me. "You want me to fuck you, don't you?"

"No," she moaned as I felt her resistance break.

I felt it was safe to let her arm go, so I released her and slid my hand into her tights. "You don't want me to fuck you, but you wet for me, huh?"

She moaned deeper as I moved my tongue across her neck and my finger over clit. Every ounce of fight left her body when I moved my finger inside of her.

"My mother is downstairs," she moaned as she opened her legs wider, allowing me better access.

"You want me to fuck you, don't you?" I spoke into her ear as my tongue moved down it.

"Shit," she moaned as I slid another finger inside of her. Her breathing was labored and forced.

I withdrew my fingers from her and quickly removed our clothes. "Since you want to put your hands on people," I said as I pinned her down.

"Key, we can't do this! My mother is downstairs."

"You should have kept your hands to yourself! I fucking warned you."

I slowly slid inside of her as her eyes rolled to the back of her head and her body tensed. Damn, I missed being inside of her. She was always wet and warm. She felt so fucking good.

"Damn, baby," I groaned as her wetness surrounded me, pulling me deeper and deeper into her. "I missed you, Tori."

She didn't reply. I knew for whatever reason she wanted to stick with being mad. I wasn't having that shit, though, not while I was inside of her.

I moved out of her slowly then back into her as deep as I could go.

"Fuck, Key," she screamed as I gripped her thighs. She placed her hand over her mouth as I moved inside of her.

"I missed you," I said again as I sped up. The headboard banged against the wall, and I knew her mother knew what was going on, but I couldn't stop, not now. "I'm sorry, Tori."

She moaned deep within her throat as I released her arms to cup her shoulders, digging as deep inside of her as I could.

"You forgive me?" I bit my lip to try to fight off what being inside of her was doing to me.

"Yes," she moaned, digging her fingers into my back.

"You love me?"

"Yes, I love you, Key. I love you so much."

"You coming home?" I asked as I sped up inside her. She didn't respond. The only thing I got was a loud moan and my name being whispered in my ear.

"Answer me, Tori," I said, tapping the deepest parts of her.

"Key, please."

"You wanna cum on this dick?"

"Yes! Please, Key! Please!"

I lifted up and wrapped her legs around my arm as I dug deeper into her. Her legs shook uncontrollably as her orgasm crashed into her.

"Stop fucking moving," I groaned as I gripped her thighs tighter as she kept shaking.

Her moans made my dick grow harder inside of her. She gripped the sheets in a death grip as her body continued to convulse. I could tell she was trying not to moan, but I wasn't having that shit. I needed to hear her. I needed to know she felt me. Felt how much I fucking loved her. She tried to squeeze her legs shut as another orgasm hit her.

"Open your fucking legs!"

"I can't! Key, Fuckkk," she cried out.

"Open them muthafuckas, Tori," I demanded as I sped up inside her.

"I fucking can't, Key," she moaned as her body went into overdrive. I had to slow down to watch that shit.

"Come on this dick then," I whispered as I felt her muscles contract around me.

"Oh, fuck! Oh, fuck!" she cried out with every jerk her body made. Her eyes were closed, and her head was thrown back. I watched the muscles in her perfect stomach clench as she grabbed the sheets tighter. Her moans almost got to me, so I did all I could to block them out. I kept moving as much as she would allow me before I came to a complete stop to just watch her. I missed watching her cum. I didn't want another mutherfucka to ever have a front-row seat to this shit. I needed to be the only man created to ever view it. It was mines. She belonged to me.

"I need you to come home, Tori," I groaned as I felt the spasms leave her body. "Do you hear me?"

She nodded weakly as her eyes closed.

Chapter 24

Winter

Graduation

I leaned against the wall in the bedroom as Demarco put his finishing touches on. He looked so good. I placed my cap on my head as he turned to me, smiling proudly.

"That's so fucking sexy, Winter," he said, walking over to me. "I wanna rip that shit off."

"By *shit* you mean my cap and gown, right?" I said, laughing at him.

"Yes."

Since the situation at the restaurant we'd tried to move forward, and I was genuinely giving it all I had. I didn't want to lose him, and I knew he did what he had to to get us out of that situation. I just wished he would tell me what the hell was going on.

He wrapped me in his arms. "I'm so proud of you, you know that?"

"Yes, I know that. You've said it twenty times."

"I just want you to know. I can't wait for the hotel to open and have you as the manager. I know fools gon' fall up in there just to see yo' fine ass, but you all mines! My Winter Storm."

My eyebrows rose to the ceiling. "That wasn't bad, Mr. Montgomery. You've been working on your romance I see."

"I have," he confessed. "I want to be romantic just to be romantic and no other reason."

I smiled at him as I kissed him. "Then I'm very proud of you."

"Thank you," he said, smiling down at me. "Do you have everything?"

"Yes," I said, grabbing my purse. "I'm ready!"

"Cool," he said, kissing my forehead. "We have to get over to Key's. That's where we meeting up since it's closest to the stadium."

I crossed my arms over my chest. "When are you giving me my graduation present, though?"

He looked at me, confused. "I did that last night," he said confidently.

I rolled my eyes. "That was not a present," I said, smirking at him.

"But you said you loved it," he said, kissing me.

"I do love that shit," I said, giggling like a schoolgirl. "But I need a real-life present."

He laughed as he released me. "I ain't got shit for you."

"You better have something, or Winter Storm will no longer be in operation after today."

His eyes got big. "You doing it like that, closing shop on a nigga? Damn, you a cold piece."

"Call it what you want," I said as I walked around him to go out of the door. I gasped when I looked in the driveway and saw an all-black 2015 Bentley Continental GT coupe with a red bow on the hood sitting in the driveway. I screamed and jumped up and down as I ran to the car. "This is mines?" I screamed at Demarco as he held the key out.

"All yours." He smiled as he stepped off the porch.

I ran over to him and wrapped my arms around his neck. "Oh, my God, Demarco. I thought you didn't get me anything!"

"That would be wack as fuck of me, Winter. I'm always gon' take care of you."

"I love you so much," I said into his neck. Again, he just tensed and held me tighter before letting me go.

After an awkward moment of silence, he walked over to the car and took the ribbon off. "You driving."

Chapter 25

TaNia

"Lemonte, we gon' be late," I moaned as he pushed me on the couch and pulled my panties to the side.

"Ten minutes," he said as he entered me roughly.

"Fuck," I groaned as I pulled my gown up and out of the way. "You say that every time, and it's always more than ten."

"Shit," he groaned as he smacked my ass. "I promise just ten this time."

I gripped the couch as he moved behind me, making the couch move with each motion he made. I spread my legs wider, causing my heels to scratch the hardwood floor as he grabbed my ass cheeks and spread them apart.

"Oh fuck, TaNia." His groan filled the air as our bodies rocked in sync.

"Lemonte," I tried pleading with him as I felt myself get wetter around him. "We have to get to . . ." I spoke between strokes.

"Cum on this dick, TaNia," he groaned again, smacking my ass.

My body was forced to give in to the things that he was doing to me. I moaned deep in my throat as he grabbed a handful of my hair and pulled it gently. "Don't mess my hair. Oh fuck," I moaned as he moved deeper into me.

"Fuck yo' hair," he growled as he slammed into me.

"Yeah, fuck this hair," I mumbled as my body began to shake. "Mon, I'm coming."

"There it goes," he groaned as he slammed into me faster.

"I'm not gon' make it," I moaned as I squeezed my eyes shut and let my orgasm take over. "Shit," I yelled as my legs shook, almost giving out. My eyes rolled as I bit into my bottom lip.

Mon grabbed me and flexed his hips, hitting my spot and only intensifying my orgasm. I grabbed the cushion of the couch as I felt him cum inside me. "I love you," I heard his groan.

"I love you too," I mumbled incoherently. "I can't move."

"You shouldn't have said that shit to me, and we would be halfway to Key's," he said, out of breath as he pulled out of me. He smacked my ass again as he walked off into his bathroom.

"I only said you look nice," I mumbled when I heard him return to the living room with a towel to wipe me off.

"It's the voice you said it in and the way you looked at me when you said it," he said as he finished cleaning me off and fixed my clothes. "So if you walking across the stage with a limp," he said as he pulled me up and turned me to face him, "that ain't my fault."

I pushed my hair to the back as I adjusted my cap on my head. "You almost knocked my cap off," I said, smiling at him.

"Congratulations, baby girl." He kissed my lips. "I'm so proud of you."

"Thank you," I replied, adjusting my gown. "Can we go now?"

"Yes," he said, smiling at me.

"What are you smiling for?"

"Because I love you and I'm lucky as fuck." He grabbed me around my waist.

"I love you way more, Lemonte."

"I doubt that shit," he said as he slipped something into my hand. I looked down at the box, then back up to him.

"What is this?"

"Open it," he said, still smiling.

"Lemonte," I whined. "Just tell me what it is."

"Nope."

I glared at him for a moment before I lifted the box up to open it. In it sat a very beautiful necklace.

"Graduated diamond eternity white gold necklace. I got it specially made for you. Happy graduation day," he said, smiling.

I didn't even want to touch it. That's how beautiful it was. "How much was this?" I asked, still looking down at it, unable to take my eyes off.

"I'm not telling you."

"Please tell me."

He exhaled as he took the box from my hand. "Why, nosy?"

"Because I want to know, Mon," I said, turning around and pulling my hair up. Can I wear it now? To graduation? What do you think? You think it'll be too much?"

"I think you can do whatever the fuck you want," he said as he placed it around my neck. It was heavy. I knew it was expensive.

"Don't lose my box," I said, turning back around and running to look at myself in the mirror. "Oh, my God, Lemonte. It's so beautiful I'm scared to wear it."

"You deserve it, TaNia. You deserve it and much more." He walked up behind me and kissed my cheek. "I love you."

"How much was it?"

He smirked before he walked off toward the door. "It was a little over sixteen thousand."

"Sixteen thousand dollars," I said in disbelief as I followed him.

"Yes. Now come on," he said over his shoulder as he walked out the door.

Chapter 26

Tori

"I don't know what the fuck you want me to do, Tori."

I shook my head and sat down at on the edge of the bed as Keyton and I argued for what seemed like the millionth time. I didn't want to argue with him, but some shit just couldn't be avoided. I could yell until I was blue in the face, and he would never get it. He would never understand, and I wasn't going to keep trying to explain shit.

"Let's just drop it, Key," I said, waving my hands. "All we do is yell at each other, but you never hear me, and I never hear you. Our friends are in the next room, so we can wait."

"I don't understand how we keep getting here, Tori. I'm fucking trying to fix this, to fix us, but you done already checked out of this marriage! Instead of just being a woman and saying that, you run to me with all the bullshit you hear."

I stood and got in his face.

He glared at me, nostrils flared. "You bet' not put'cho muthafuckin' hands on me, because I promise on this day, I will knock yo' li'l ass out. Dead ass, ma. Don't fucking touch me!"

"Fuck you," I yelled. "Kiss my ass! Fuck you and all these hoes you fucking, and I hope you get some shit and die!"

"If I get some shit, you'll be the one to give it to me, and I'm bodying you and that nigga who gave it to you! Fuck is you talking about?"

"So she is lying like everybody else, right?"

"How many fucking times I got to tell you that?" Keyton yelled in my face, veins popping out of his neck. "These bitches want what you got, Tori. They see the shit you rock. They see the cars and shit. They come out of fucking nowhere with these made-up-ass stories, and you just eat that shit up! What this bitch tell you? She fucked? Or did she suck my dick? Oh, wait, this the bitch I gave bread to, right? Fuck outta here with that bullshit! Let me break this down for the last fucking time! I'm not fucking these hoes! I love you! My wife! My fucking backbone. And I'm tired of you believing these hoes over me! I'm fucking tired!"

"That's easy for you to say, Keyton! You don't have men coming up to you, telling you that they fucked me!"

He huffed. "You right. I don't! But you know what I would do if I did? I would tell that fuck boy he was a lying muthafucka because the woman I love would never do no shit like that to me! Then I'd body that fool for spreading lies! I'm your husband, Tori."

"And I'm your wife!"

"Act like it then," he yelled as he turned around to walk off but quickly turned back around. He grabbed a set of keys out of his pocket and pushed them into my hand. "The keys to the $1.5 million house I got built for us while you out here believing other shit! This is the only thing I been up to, Tori! This and making sure that you're safe! That's it," he said as he looked at me. "Believe it or not I love you, and I'm not cheating on you. I only want you!"

I looked down at the keys in my hand and couldn't contain my joy! "You really got a house built?"

"I told you, I'd give you anything!"

I exhaled because I immediately felt bad. "I'm sorry, Key."

He bent down in front of me. "I love you, Tori! Only you, and I promise you I'll fix this." He kissed me as he stood. "I'm gon' send Winter and Nia in here so y'all can finish getting ready. I'm proud of you, Tori."

"Thank you," I said, smiling weakly.

He walked off, and a minute later, Winter and Nia walked in.

"What the hell happened to your hair, TaNia?" I said, trying not to laugh.

She fumbled for a response. "Well I, uh . . . We rode with the windows down. Winter, you can help me out, though, right?"

Winter laughed. "Girl, that's code for Lemonte pinned that ass down! But yes, I can help."

Winter and I laughed as Nia went into the bathroom. "Where the wand curlers?" she said to me.

"Under the sink," I said, still laughing.

Winter sat down on the bed with me. "Mon was like, 'Bring that assssss here, girl!'"

"I heard that," Nia said, coming out of the bathroom with the curlers as well as the pregnancy test I got from the pharmacy earlier this week.

"Why are you going through my stuff?" I said, annoyed as I stood and snatched it from her.

"I just so happened to pull it out with the curlers. But the real question is, when are you taking it?"

I fondled with it in my hands. "I'm scared."

"Why?" Winter asked. "We're here with you. Just go take it."

I looked at them for a moment before I walked off into the bathroom.

After about ten minutes of just sitting in the bathroom, I was finally able to get the test done. I looked down at the stick in my hand as tears flowed from my eyes. "Fuck," I almost screamed as I came out of the bathroom in my cap and gown.

I looked up at Winter and TaNia, who had big grins on their faces. I rolled my eyes at them as I walked into the living room with them trailing behind me.

"So, what the stick say?" TaNia asked, already knowing the answer.

"Yeah, heffa, out with it," Winter said.

I sat down on the couch and held my face in my hands. "I can't be pregnant right now. It's the worst time!"

"Yes," TaNia said, pumping her fist. "Go Key!"

"Yes! I'm going to be an auntie," Winter yelled.

"Key and I can't even see eye to eye. We spend all day arguing. I can't bring a baby into this."

"You don't have a choice," TaNia said.

I exhaled. "I know I don't!" I lay on the couch. "Fuck my life!"

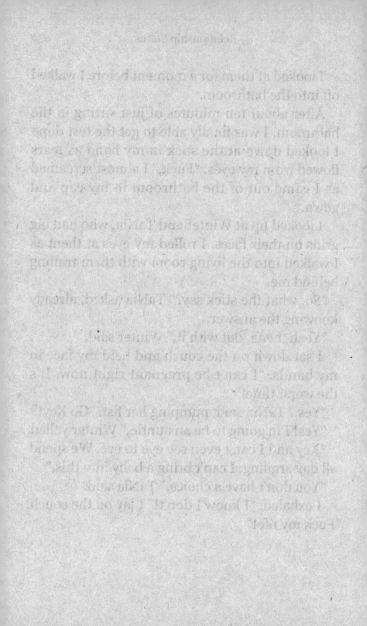

Chapter 27

TaNia

I was daydreaming. I couldn't wipe the smile off my face if I wanted to. I couldn't believe Tori was pregnant! We were all officially college graduates, and I couldn't be happier. The ladies were cooking dinner, and I was sent to the store to get the stuff. So, here I was in this long-ass Walmart line, waiting to check out.

I looked down at my phone as it vibrated in my hand. I smiled when I saw who the message was from.

Love: I can still taste you, TaNia. I can't wait to touch you.

Me: You can't text me stuff like this during the day!

Love: It's what I'm dealing with, TaNia. My dick gets hard every time I lick my lips. Food doesn't fill me up no more. I can't fucking function. I need to see you!

"This man," I whispered, looking around the store as if someone had caught me doing something dirty. Geez! I needed to change the subject.

Me: Did you go enroll in a class like we discussed?

Love: Yeah, I did. I still ain't really feeling that shit but whatever. But say, you still cooking? I'm trying to make love to you immediately after.

I wanted to fuck with him, so I laughed as I typed my reply.

Me: I got a headache.

Love: Don't start that shit, TaNia. I got something for that.

Me: I ain't feeling it tonight, Lemonte. Can we just cuddle?

Love: Yeah, TaNia.

I knew his ass wasn't going to just cuddle with me, but I wouldn't complain much since I wanted the same thing he wanted.

As soon as I paid for the stuff, I walked straight to my car. My steps slowed as I examined the glass on the ground from the busted windows. "What the fuck?" I whispered as I adjusted the bags in my hands and looked around. My heart broke just thinking about someone touching my most valued possession. This was the only material thing my dad left me, besides the money. I felt my air leave my lungs as I examined the damage. There were dents all around, the head-lights and taillights were busted out, and every single window was busted. I could see a trail of sugar where they put sugar in my tank. That was some petty shit only a bitter bitch would do. I sat down on the curb as tears gathered in my eyes. I was far from materialistic, but this car constantly reminded me of my dad, and now it was totaled.

I pulled out my phone out as I continued to cry. I called the only person I could think of.

"Yoooooo."

I couldn't even get my words out to tell him what was going on. My voice broke as I struggled to speak. "My car . . ."

"TaNia, what's wrong?"

I swallowed hard as I continued to cry. "It's destroyed, Mon. They fucking totaled my dad's car!"

"Shit," Lemonte mumbled. "Where you at?"

"I'm still at Walmart on thirty," I spoke as I removed the bags and sat them on the curb. "I had to come and get the food."

"I'm on my way! Don't move!"

"Where the fuck am I going to go, Lemonte? My fucking car is totaled!" I hung up the phone is his face. This is what I meant when I said bull-shit and drama. I didn't need this shit! I already had enough on my plate! I was still sitting on the curb crying and looking at my car when Lemonte, Key, and Tori pulled up chauffeured by Cortez ten minutes later.

Tori immediately came to me. Sitting down, she pulled me into her arms as I cried harder. Mon and Key had frowns covering their faces.

"Who the fuck would do some shit like this?" Mon asked as he walked around my car.

"Whoever it was planned this shit. There's sugar in the tank. It had to be multiple people, because ain't no fucking way no one person could get some shit like this accomplished by themselves in broad daylight in a packed-ass Walmart parking lot. Where the fuck was the rent-a-cop who patrols the ground?"

I looked up at Lemonte. I could tell he didn't know what to do or say. He couldn't even look at me, because he knew this was his fault. I was trying my hardest not to be pissed at him, but I didn't know anyone else to be mad at. He finally looked at me as me and Tori stood.

"I'm sorry—"

"Fuck that," I yelled, cutting him off. "This that bullshit, Lemonte!"

"I know, TaNia. I'm sorry, baby girl! I don't know what the fuck this is about, but I promise to get to the bottom of it. I'll get you new wheels."

"You don't get it," I said, stepping into his face. "It's not just a fucking car, Lemonte!"

"I know that, TaNia. Shit! I don't know what the fuck to do! I'll get you new wheels! I'll pay whatever to get your dad's car fixed. I'll figure it out, all right?"

I exhaled deeply as I shook my head. "I'm not doing this shit with you! It's a waste of my fucking time! How am I going to explain this to my mom? She is going to flip the hell out!"

Tori walked over to me and grabbed my hand. "Come on, TaNia. Get in the car. Mon and Key will figure it out!"

She ice grilled them both before she pulled me to the car. I didn't resist, because honestly, I didn't have the strength to. Cortez nodded at me as he opened my door. Usually, we would at least exchange verbal greetings, but today he didn't say anything. I could see that he was pissed off, but he didn't speak. The entire situation was tense.

I sat in the back of the Escalade in my thoughts. What Keyton said made sense. Where the hell was the patrol? They were always here, patrolling the grounds, watching shoppers, and checking on things like this. It was weird that they were nowhere to be found. It was Walmart! Always packed and crowded! Someone had to see this!

There was no way they didn't see this shit go down when it did.

"I'm sure your mom will understand, Nia. Keyton will get it fixed. It will be okay."

I looked at Tori and half smiled. I knew she was trying to reassure me, but I had a feeling my dad's car was the tip of the iceberg. I knew it was planned out and executed. It was personal. Just like that shit at the restaurant with Marco. Whoever was after them was coming for us too. It had to be someone who knew me and what that car meant to me. It was all just too much!

"I don't feel like it's over, Tori. I mean, I don't want to bring it up, but what if it's the same type of thing you went through? I'm not as tough as you, Tori." I felt fresh tears form in my eyes as I thought about what my friend went through. I remembered how much it broke her. She still wasn't the same. She lost her child and required physical rehabilitation from the attack. Those bitches were weak and waited until she was alone to come at her. "I could never survive no shit like that," I said as tears slid down my face.

Tori sat across from me with her head down. I knew she still dealt with that shit daily. She talked to me about her fears of starting a family and the nightmares she had. "I'm sorry, Tor. I shouldn't have—"

"You're not bringing up something if it's constantly on my fucking mind anyway," she spoke in a somber tone. "Lemonte would never let anything like that happen to you."

I looked at her as if she were crazy. "You think if anything that happened to you were in Keyton's control he would've allowed that to happen? That shit destroyed him too, Tori. I saw him cry. Keyton never cries."

She nodded. "Deep down I know that. I just can't help but blame him. I think I'm falling out of love with him."

I was not expecting her to say that! "What?"

Chapter 28

Tori

Shit! I didn't mean to let that come out.

I looked to the front of the car as Keyton and Lemonte spoke to the man with the tow truck. How could you love a person and feel like you hated them at the same time? I wanted to love him. I wanted that to be the only thing I felt, but deep down I hated him. I wanted my daughter. I wanted to see her grow up and call me Mommy. I would never get that. I just wanted her! I looked over at Nia, who looked so beautiful even though she was crying and upset. The confused expression covering her tear-filled face made my heart break.

"It's not important," I said, still looking at him. "I'm dealing with it."

TaNia looked at me, frowning. "I don't understand what's going on with you. You have been in love with Key—"

"I know how long I've been in love with him, Nia. I've tried to get over this shit, but it's not easy!"

I looked up when Keyton opened the door to the truck and climbed in. "Why are you crying?"

I knew that would be the first question he asked me. "I'm fine."

He frowned as he wiped my face. "But that's not what I asked you."

I pushed his hand away and licked my lips before I wiped my own face. "I said I'm fine! What did the man say?"

"He towing the car to my body shop," Keyton said, looking at Nia, who had her head turned looking out the window. "Baby." He reached out to touch me, and I pushed his hand away. He looked at me for a long time before he sat back in his seat and released a deep breath.

The tension in the car was so thick. No one spoke, but I could tell that each of us had a whole lot to say. Keyton wouldn't take his eyes off of me. I could feel him staring at me though I was looking down. We sat there as Cortez drove around with no destination for about thirty minutes. I looked up, and Keyton was texting on his phone. It was clear he was texting Mon, because he was nodding.

"I would like to get some rest," I said, breaking the silence.

Keyton looked up at me. "Okay, baby. I have something I need to run by you and Nia."

I looked at Nia, who didn't budge. "What's up?" I asked, looking back at Key.

"I think we need a vacation. I know we do, Tori."

"We can't go on vacation. The hotel opens in two weeks."

"I know. That's the thing I wanted to talk to y'all about—"

"Fuck no," Nia interrupted while shaking her head. "Do you know how much work needs to be done before opening? Going anywhere is going to set everything back."

"You gon' do whatever the fuck is necessary," Mon said, cutting Nia off. "I don't give a fuck about nothing else but your safety. I feel the need for us to take a vacation, so that's what the fuck we doing. You pissed off. I get it. But be fucking smart."

"I was fucking smart until I start fucking with yo' ass," Nia said, getting in his face.

"Sit'cho ass the fuck back and chill out," Mon yelled, getting back in hers. "You better calm the hell down. I don't know who the fuck you think you talking to!"

"TaNia, chill out," I said, looking at her as she bounced her legs and crossed her arms over her chest.

"Better listen to your best friend if you know what the fuck is best for you. Lower your motherfucking voice," Mon spoke.

"Nia, it has to happen, baby girl," Keyton said, looking at her.

"She good," Mon said, fuming. "We tried it y'all way and the shit didn't work, so it is what it is."

TaNia looked at Key a moment before she turned and looked back out the window.

"Like right now, Key?" I asked, looking at him.

"We could go home and get some things and leave. I know you're tired, but you can sleep on the plane. We can grab something to eat before the driver drops us off."

I shook my head as I looked out the window. "Where are we going?"

"Turks and Caicos," Mon said in a voice that indicated that he was still very much pissed.

I almost jumped out of my seat. I looked over at Nia, who had a huge smile on her face. "Turks and Caicos," I half screamed. "I always wanted to go there."

"I know, so that's why we're taking y'all. It's actually a graduation gift."

"We'll have to figure this out, because I don't want to get behind when it comes to the opening, but Turks and Caicos sounds hella good!"

"I'll handle all that," Keyton said, grabbing my hand. He looked into my eyes, and I wanted so badly to feel what I always felt, but I didn't. That reality made my heart break. "I know what's been going on with you, Tori. I know that you don't love me the way you used to. I also know that you blame me for the things that happened to you, but I can't lose you. I won't say that I don't feel some type of way about things, but I can't help but fight for you. You all I know."

I looked up at Keyton with tears in my eyes. I couldn't deal with this shit right now. We were in two different places. Here I was fighting to love, and my best friend was fighting against it. "I love you, Keyton."

He shook his head and gave me a half smile. "I know."

I bowed my head as the truck came to a stop in front of Nia's house. Both she and Mon got out and walked up the steps to her house.

Keyton continued to look at me intently. "I wanna fix this, Tori. Whatever I gotta do, I'll do it."

I nodded. What the fuck was wrong with me? I was so frustrated with myself, and I couldn't shake what I was feeling, but I knew I still loved him. I knew I still needed him. "I don't know what's wrong with me," I spoke softly as I looked at him. "I've tried to forget, to move on, Keyton. I just can't stop thinking about it."

"Tell me. Tell me what you think about."

I looked at him for a moment before I spoke. "I called you," I said as my voice broke. "I screamed for you to help me," I said as unshed tears caught my words in my throat. "I screamed for you to help us, but you never came. They said you didn't give a fuck about me and that it was your fault. They said you didn't love me, Keyton. I didn't want to believe them, but you never came."

I cried as I bent down and grabbed my head, running my hands through my hair. "I'm fucked up." I cried louder as he grabbed me, pulling me into his lap. I cried against him as he held me tight, pulling me as close to him as I could get. I didn't know why I was breaking down even a year after everything that happened. Before I could finish that thought, I knew why. It was because I never really dealt with it. I never healed. I never talked to anyone about it, not even Nia. I never got over it because I was still living it.

Chapter 29

Lemonte

I was pissed the fuck off. I wanted to run my hand through the fucking wall, but I knew that wouldn't get me anywhere. To see Nia crying her eyes out over her father's car almost killed me. I never knew I could love another human being as much as I loved Nia. She was so much a part of me that when she hurt, I felt that shit. Right now, shorty was in so much pain, and I couldn't do anything to help her.

I was sort of relieved when we pulled up and her mother wasn't home. I needed time to wrap my head around shit before I could talk to Mrs. Diane. I knew she wasn't going to take the news well. I was going to get the car repaired, but I understood why Nia was so pissed. I couldn't imagine what she was feeling right now. I stood on the other side of her room as she walked around, packing, all the while shooting me looks that would kill me if they were able to.

She packed her things with no urgency. She wouldn't be rushed, and I wasn't in a position to say shit, so I just chuckled and shook my head.

She stopped walking altogether and looked at me. "You got something to say?"

I shook my head and held my hands up in surrender. "Not shit. I'm just waiting for you, baby girl."

"You gon' wait, too," she said, placing her hands on her thick hips.

Those shits were looking right, but I had to focus on getting us the hell out of here. "It's your world, beautiful."

She slowly resumed packing as she continued to look at me. *Sexy ass. She better hurry the hell up before I pin her ass down.*

"I'm not gon' keep going through this shit, Mon."

I exhaled and shook my head. "Here we go."

"Yes! Here we go! I'm serious. The one thing I asked you for is to be honest and upfront about your shit. I don't do drama! I don't get into shit. I'm low-key, but since messing with you, it's like drama follows me."

"I asked you to stay low-key."

She squinted her eyes at me. "Let me find out one of these girls you mess around with is behind this, Mon. I'm gon' fuck you and that bitch up."

"So what the hell you want from me, Nia? I can't fucking control the universe and prevent things from happening. The only thing I can do is protect you to the best of my ability. I told you it was hot. I practically begged you to stay low-key, but no, yo' ass," I said, stepping in her face, "Ms. Independent, 'I don't need a nigga fa shit' Nia wanted to do things her own way. See how that shit didn't work? 'I don't need a guard dog! I don't need shit.'"

She held her head down and bounced her leg, pissed off because she knew I was right. "Yes," she mumbled. She could save that pouting shit, because I wasn't falling for that shit today. *Spoiled ass.*

"You can stop all that pouting shit! It ain't working this time!"

"I ain't pouting," she said, sticking her bottom lip out.

I flicked my finger across it. "What you call it?"

Between the voice and the puppy-dog eyes, she got my ass. I exhaled as I grabbed her hand and pulled her to me. "I'm sorry for yelling."

"I just want you to listen to me," she said, pouting harder. "That was my dad's car, Mon. What if they can't fix it?"

"They'll fix it. It's all body damage. They would just need to drop the tank to get the sugar out.

Besides that, it's all body damage, which can always be repaired."

She nodded as she stepped around me. I turned to look at her as she began packing again. I sat on the edge of her bed and exhaled. I was already drained from this shit. I needed to get to the bottom of it before it got out of hand. I couldn't continue to worry about Nia every time she was out of my sight and handle business at the same time. I needed some type of balance.

I felt her walk in front of me and place her hands on my shoulder. Damn, she smelled good.

"I'm not trying to stress you out, Mon."

I reached up to grab her thick thighs as I rested my head on her stomach. She was the relief I needed to deal with all this shit. I couldn't imagine rocking with anyone else but her. She was all I needed.

"I know, baby," I said as I grabbed her hand to kiss it.

She ran her fingers through my dreads, soothing me, and I kissed her. TaNia was irreplaceable.

"I'm scared, Lemonte."

To hear her softly confess the very thing I feared fucked with me. I didn't want her worried about this shit. I wanted her to know that I would always have her, always be there to protect her. "You ain't gotta worry about shit." I stood up and wrapped my arms around her. "You with me, TaNia. I'll do everything in my power to protect you at all times, by any means." I grabbed her face so she could look into my eyes. "Do you understand that?"

"Yes," she mumbled as she nodded. "I know that. It's just—"

I leaned down to kiss her because it was what I needed. It was what I felt she needed. I let my tongue caress hers as my hands moved around to grab her ass. She reached up and wrapped her arms around me, playing in my dreads like she always did. I loved kissing her. Her lips melted against mine, and her body felt like cotton. I heard her moan, and that in itself made my dick hard. I knew I had to be patient with her, but I couldn't wait to feel all of her.

I ended the kiss when I heard the horn being blown outside. TaNia continued to plant kisses all over my face and neck, still holding me as if she didn't have a care in the world.

I caught her lips when she moved to kiss my cheek, and I kissed her again, grabbing more of her ass and pulling her against me. She moaned deeper and pulled more of my dreads into her hands. "I love you so much," she moaned against my lips.

Shit! I needed to get us out of here before I made love to her and held everybody up. "I love you too, TaNia. Always know that." I spoke softly in between kisses. "Come on, we have to go."

"But I want you, Mon."

I didn't realize she had my dick in her hands until it was too fucking late. "TaNia, Key gon' kill us," I said as I turned her around and laid her on the bed. I lay on top of her as she moved her legs apart so that I could fall between them. She released me to move her hands up my back, putting my shirt up. "We can't right now, ma. We got a plane to catch."

She wasn't listening. I felt her soft hands unbuckling my pants as she continued to kiss me, softly running her tongue across my lobe. "Just make me cum," she whispered as she continued to run her hands across my back. She didn't understand how fucking sexy she was, from her body to her voice and the way she felt. I couldn't get past the way she smelled or the way she moaned my name when she wanted something. Like she was fucking doing now.

"Make you cum," I asked her, giving in. I had to give baby what she asked for. I moved my hands down the center of her body, cupping her pussy through her clothes.

"Please, Lemonte," she moaned close to my ear.

I moved my hand to slide over her pants to reach into her panties. She clung to me as if she thought I would move. "We can't make love. We have to go get Marco and Winter. I'll make you cum now, then fuck you on the beach in Turks and Caicos," I moaned as I slid my finger over her clit. She released a moan as she opened her legs wider to give me access. "That's what you want, right?"

"Yes, baby, please," she moaned in my ear as I slid two fingers inside her. She was so tight and warm, but her wetness allowed my fingers to glide inside of her smoothly. She placed soft kisses on my neck as she moved her hips to get closer to me. Her scent tickled my nose as I buried my face in her neck, sucking softly as my other hand gripped her breast through her shirt.

Before I knew it, she was creaming all over my hand. I wanted so bad to get inside of her, but we had somewhere to be.

Chapter 30

Winter

"Turks and Caicos?" I asked as I watched Marco throw my things into my suitcase.

"Yes," he said without looking up.

I blew air through my lips and continued looking at him. "For how long?"

"A week."

The first thing that popped into my mind was that I definitely was excited about Turks and Caicos, but I wanted to know why we were going. "Any reason we leaving so suddenly?"

"Winter," he said as he stopped packing. "Can you chill with the questions right now? Damn," he mumbled in a frustrated tone as he returned to packing my bag.

"What the hell, Demarco?" I said, walking up to him. He shook his head as he stood straight to face me. I looked up at him, and he looked stressed out. I didn't understand the sudden mood change. We were just chilling and watching movies before he received that phone call. Now he was back in defense mode and blocking me out. "Talk to me," I said, grabbing his arm.

He snatched away from me, causing me to flinch and take a step back. "Look, Winter. Not right now. The only thing I need you to do is help me get your shit together so we can be ready when Key and Mon get here. Can you fucking do that?"

I looked at him as if he had lost his mind. He never yelled at me, not once since I'd been knowing him. Even when I was spazzing and yelling at the top of my lungs, he was always calm and collected. To say I was pissed that he was yelling at me would be an understatement. I was hurt.

"Don't fucking yell at me, Demarco," I said, looking at him. He turned to look at me as if he was about to yell again, until he saw me. I was on the verge of tears. I hated being yelled at. It brought up too many memories of my childhood. My dad would come in yelling at all of us in his drunken state, then he'd beat my mother until she was unrecognizable. I promised myself at a young age that I would never allow a man to do that to me, and I would never change that.

He exhaled as he reached out to touch me, but I moved back from him. "I'm not going anywhere with you while you're like this, Demarco."

He bit his lip as if he wanted to go off again then thought better of it. "I'm sorry, Winter. I just need you to get your things so we can go and not ask me questions right now, baby. I can explain everything on the plane. Will you just trust me for once? Please?"

I didn't understand the urgency, which was the reason I was confused. Why all of a sudden did we need to leave? "Fine," I said reluctantly.

I walked past him and out of my room. As much as I was feeling Demarco, I was completely thrown off by him sometimes. I didn't understand what he wanted from me. I mean, he pursued me just to get into this relationship and be closed out and guarded. I was falling in love with him, and honestly, I was scared as hell. I did everything he asked me to do. He wanted me to quit dancing so that I could manage the hotel when it opened, and he even gave me an advance of $20,000 to hold me over until the opening. I knew deep down inside that he had to have some type of feelings toward me. I mean, I felt it when he touched me. Every time we kissed or hugged, it showed. I felt it, but every time I said it to him he would tense up and completely avoid saying it back or even acknowledging that I said it. This relationship has been nothing but giving emotionally on my end and giving financially on his. I didn't need his money, though. I needed his heart.

"You mad at me," I heard him say as I reached into the refrigerator to grab a bottle of water.

I looked over at him as I turned to the counter to get a napkin. "It doesn't matter if I am, Demarco, because all you're going to do is tell me a million reasons why I shouldn't be."

"You act like I don't give a fuck about how you feel, Winter."

"Do you?" I asked, turning to him. "If you do, I wasn't aware. You treat me like a piece of property versus the woman who makes love to you. I'm sick of that shit. You tell me to jump, and I'm just supposed to say how high without knowing anything else? That's unfair."

He rubbed a hand down his waves as he shook his head. "What do you want from me?"

"I want you to listen, Demarco. To care for something or someone other than yourself!"

"You think I don't care about you?" he said, walking over to me. His voice was low, but I could tell he was pissed off. "How can you think that?"

"Well, let me think. When was the last time you told me you cared? You sure as hell never said anything about love, and I get it, Demarco, I really do. But that doesn't stop me from loving you and wanting to be with you. What I won't do, though, is be with someone who doesn't value me as his woman."

"I value you, Winter. It's just this love thing is too much. I care about you a whole hell of a lot, and I don't wanna lose you."

I nodded as I went to walk past him. He grabbed me and pulled me into him. "I'm sorry, baby. Just be patient with me."

I chuckled as I stepped out of his embrace. "Story of my life: Winter waiting," I said as I walked back up the stairs. "I'm going to finish packing."

Something kept telling me that I was wasting my time with Demarco. It was like trying to love a brick wall. The minute I thought he may be letting me in, he would shut me right back out. As I sat in the private jet, I started to feel out of place. Keyton and Tori seemed to be in a very deep conversation, TaNia and Mon were all over each other, and I sat across from Demarco, but I felt as if I could still be in Dallas and he wouldn't have noticed.

I listened to Jhené Aiko sing about sailing out as the clouds in the sky took me away mentally. I pulled the blanket covering my body up to my face as I continued to glance out the window. After a moment, I felt my earphones being pulled out. I removed the blanket to look over at a smiling Demarco. I rolled my eyes and sat up. "Is there a reason you took my headphones out?"

"We on our way to Turks and Caicos and you're ignoring me."

I exhaled deeply as I pulled my legs up in the seat. "It's better when we ignore each other, Demarco."

He laughed as he moved to sit beside me. "Stop being mean to me," he fake pouted, giving me puppy-dog eyes. I looked at him sideways and pulled the cover back over me. I felt his hand touch my ass, and I couldn't help the blush that spread across my face.

I looked back at him, and he was still smiling super hard. "Don't start, Demarco," I whispered.

He leaned in closer and gripped my ass tighter. He moved my cover back so that he could slide under it with me. "You gon' let me fuck you on the beach of Turks and Caicos?" he asked in my ear as his hand moved around to touch me intimately.

"No," I said, making a half-hearted attempt at pushing his hand back.

"Quit playing," he said as he successfully found his way to my womanhood. "You ain't gon' let me make love to you on the beach, though? You can ride this dick while the water washes over us."

I covered my mouth as I laughed out loud. "Demarco, is that supposed to sound romantic? Because you failing horribly."

He buried his face in my neck. "That is romantic."

"No, it's not," I moaned as I felt his fingers caress my clit.

"It got you wet though," he cooed against my neck.

"That's by default," I murmured as I turned my head to kiss him. He tasted so good, and he smelled even better. I closed my eyes as I ran my fingers through his beard. The fact that not even an hour ago I wanted to shoot him was no longer a factor. That was the type of control he had over me. I wanted to make love to him right here and now. It didn't matter that there were two other couples on this small plane.

Chapter 31

Keyton

I placed the last of luggage in the closet as I turned to look at Tori. She was looking out the window at the beach below us. We decided to stay at a beach-front hotel so that we could have easy access. I didn't know what I needed to do to make things right with Tori, but I knew that I wasn't giving up on her. I couldn't imagine life without her, and I honestly didn't want to. Having her away from me for any amount of time fucked me up. The things that she revealed to me in the car really fucked me up. I blamed myself for not protecting her and our child. Trust me when I say I lived with it every day. I didn't want to face the fact that I was losing the only thing that ever mattered to me, but I loved her too much to keep her in a loveless marriage. If she felt like another man was what she needed to be happy, then I would just have to deal with that.

"You need anything?" I asked as I took a few steps toward her.

She looked back at me and shook her head as her gaze returned to the waves of the ocean. "It's so beautiful here, Key. Thank you for bringing me."

I walked up behind her and wrapped my hands around her waist. I placed a kiss on her cheek as I squeezed her tighter. "Anything for you, beautiful."

She turned to me and looked into my eyes. "I don't want to lose us."

I gave her a half smile. "Man, who you telling? I don't want to lose you, Tori, but I want you to be happy, ma. Even if I'm not the man helping to supply that happiness."

I watched her eyes fill with tears, and I wiped them away before they could fall. "I love you, Tori Dior. I always will."

"I wish I could just forget, Key," she cried, looking up at me.

I placed a kiss on her lips as I pushed her hair back from her face. "I can promise you this, baby girl. If I lose you, my life won't be the same. I'm going to do everything I can to make sure that I don't."

She inhaled deeply as she released me to wipe her face. "I shouldn't be crying. We are in this beautiful place for an entire week. What are we going to do?"

I knew what I wanted to spend my time doing, but I knew she wasn't going to be down for that. Not for an entire week, but I needed to get her ass pregnant as soon as possible. Hopefully, this island would bring us some luck.

"Well, I know the first thing we're doing is going to the beach."

"Yes," she said, cheering up. "I'm so ready!"

I smiled at her. "Well, put on your bathing suit. I'll wait in here."

I watched her ass as she walked into the bathroom. I sat on the bed, consumed by my thoughts. We had to find out who was trying to off us. I made sure to place a full security detail around Tori's parents. Every time they left the house as well as while they were at home, they had security. I wasn't taking any chances.

We needed this getaway because, for some reason, I felt hell coming.

We would just enjoy paradise for now.

Chapter 32

Keyton

The Grand Opening

I was on cloud nine. I let my eyes move down Tori as she talked to Nia and Winter as if I weren't standing there. She looked so beautiful in her white Carly Cushnie dress that curved to every slope and curve of her slim frame. She was looking a lot thicker these days, and I wasn't complaining one bit. I didn't give a fuck if she gained a hundred pounds. She was all mine, and that was all that mattered.

"We out," Marco said as he raised his glass to the sky. His low voice was raised as he smiled hard. I had to smile back and raise my glass for the toast. We all toasted and let out manly shouts as we started moving to the music that was playing low in the background. The lobby was full of people who already had rooms booked for the week and future dates. We would be at full capacity for a while before we could open the calendar back up. Three Kings was the place to be, from the spa and fitness room on the main level to the theater room and indoor pool on to top level and ceiling. The rooms were complete with a mini-fridge and sitting area in each one, golden accessories, and Jacuzzi-style tubs and steam showers. All of us owned a suite on the top floor that could only be rented out with our approval.

Winter was the manager, with TaNia as her assistant, while Tori handled the accounting aspect. The ladies ran a tight ship. They had maids who catered to the guests during their stay. Some specialized maids stayed on each floor to be of immediate assistance if needed. Outside of that, we had a full bar that was constantly tended by trained mixologists and bartenders. Three Kings was upscale, classy, and on its way to becoming a great asset to the downtown Dallas area. On top of all that, it was owned by three black men.

"I'm about to go to the restroom real quick. I'll be right back," Mon said, setting his glass on the table and stepping away. He staggered a little bit as if he were drunk, but the night was young, and we hadn't had much to drink.

"Say, Mon. You all right?"

"I feel lightheaded as fuck. I don't know what the hell I'm tripping on, but I'm about to go try splashing some water on my face or something. I know I ain't that fucking lit this early."

Marco laughed. "I was about to say, when the hell you turn into a lightweight, my boy?"

Mon laughed. "Never that. That's how I know I'm tripping."

"Well, you need me to go with you?" I was looking at him suspiciously. What Marco said was true. Mon could hold his liquor better than any of us, so to see him drunk after just a few drinks was not normal.

"I'm good," he said, grabbing his head. "I'll be right back."

"This is such a turn-on," I heard Tori whisper in my ear only for me to hear. I turned to look at her as my smile deepened. She had her hair in these huge curls with dark, barely noticeable purple highlights. I ran my hands through it as I bent down to kiss her.

"I love you."

"I love you way more," she said, kissing me again. I was so glad I had the woman I first fell in love with in the hallway of our high school. I felt the love that she had for me every time she got within ten feet of me. That was what I needed to get by. She provided it so freely now, and I would never ever take it for granted again.

"I can't wait to get to this suite, though," I said as I gripped her ass. "You gon' moan my name while I'm deep inside of you, putting babies in that ass as you look over downtown Dallas."

"Promises," she said, kissing my cheek.

I was so wrapped up looking into her eyes that I didn't feel TaNia tap me. "Look, y'all cute or whatever, but I'm trying to see what this spa about, like tonight."

I laughed at her as I released Tori. "The spa is closed, TaNia. It's open from nine a.m. to nine p.m. It's not twenty-four hours."

"The hell?" she asked, frowning. "I need my back rubbed and a foot massage."

"Where is Mon? That's his job," Tori said, smiling.

"He went to the restroom. He got lit too soon, so I think he throwing up," I spoke up for my boy.

"No," TaNia said, frowning. "I just need a back rub and a foot massage. That fool gon' be all extra trying to hit, and I ain't feeling that tonight. I need a break."

"What?" I said, smiling. "You gon' do my boy like that on the grand opening night? That's foul, TaNia."

Tori and Nia shared a laughed as Winter walked up. "Congratulations, gentlemen. I'm super proud of y'all!"

"No, for real, though. Y'all doing it. I can't even front on y'all," TaNia said, looking at Marco and me. "But, let me go find my baby and help his drunk ass," she said as she walked off.

Chapter 33

Lemonte

I stumbled into the first bathroom I could find, which happened to be a bathroom open to the public. I was so glad it was empty, outside of the attendant who was paid to just sit there and offer extra toiletries, even condoms if need be.

"Shit," I groaned as I grabbed a heated towel and cautiously placed it over my face. I grabbed the sleeve of my all-black Armani suit jacket and tugged it off, hanging it on the coat rack. I ran my finger around the front of my tie loop to loosen it up and removed the band that was holding my dreads together, letting them fall into my face. I was supposed to be enjoying the opening, but for some reason, I couldn't pull myself out of this cloud I was in. I needed to get myself together so I could go mingle with our future customers and grope on TaNia.

"Say," I said to the attendant. "You got some aspirin or some shit?" I asked the attendant as I looked at him.

"Of course, Mr. Reed," he said as he stood and went to the medicine cabinet.

"Do you have a headache, boss?" I heard someone speak from the door.

I looked over as the attendant reached into the medicine cabinet and pulled out a BC Powder. Delia seductively took it out of his hands and smiled at him. The older man looked as if he were about to faint. "Do me a favor," she said to him. "Stand at the door and make sure no one enters."

She pulled a hundred-dollar bill from her breast and handed it to him. He smiled as if he won the lottery and nodded quickly before he walked out of the door.

I looked around, confused because I knew this was the men's restroom.

"I'll take care of this," she told the attendant as he walked out.

I squinted as my vision began to blur. "Delia, fuck is you doing in the men's restroom?" I was laughing, but I didn't know what the fuck I was laughing for.

"You asked me to come, remember?" she said. "You said you wanted to fuck me in the bathroom of your new hotel."

I laughed again as I stumbled in my stance. "When the fuck I say that?"

She smiled at me as she began to walk toward me. "You just did."

I wanted to stop her from touching me, but I needed to fucking sit down. She pushed me back into the lounge chair that sat in the corner of the bathroom before she straddled me.

"Oh shit," I said as my head fell back on the cushion of the couch. She felt so good on top of me. Her scent made my dick hard as she reached to remove my belt. "Delia," I mumbled as my mind became more clouded, "I'm drunk as fuck."

She laughed at me and shook her head. "No, Lemonte. You're drugged as fuck, and now you will fuck me."

I heard what she said, and in my mind, I pushed her snake ass off me, but in reality, she was pulling my dick from my pants. "What the fuck you do, Delia?"

"Your dick is bigger than I dreamt it would be, but I can handle him. Oh, and what I did?" she said as she let out the craziest laugh I ever heard. "Rohypnol, the date rape drug, and a small amount of ecstasy, so I can make sure you stay up. I don't work well with a limp dick. By that time, my team will be in place."

She pulled a Magnum out of nowhere and placed it on my dick as she rose up and slid down on top of me.

"Oh fuck," I groaned as she began to ride me. "We gon' fucking die," I mumbled.

"Tell me you love me," she moaned in my ear. "Smack my ass and tell me."

I knew she was crazy at this point, but my limbs wouldn't move to fight her off. I couldn't even see straight. "TaNia," I mumbled as she began to ride me faster. She was loud as fuck, screaming my name and bouncing on top of me.

"Yes, daddy! Call me TaNia! Tell me you love me," she said as she continued to move. "Does her pussy get wet like this, huh? Do you know how many times I wanted to come into that office and fuck you, but I had to do a job? I had to learn everything I could about your operation. I had to get in good with you so we could take y'all down. But I wasn't supposed to fuck you. He is probably going to kill me, but I don't give a fuck. We'll die together."

I had to get the fuck away from her, but the moment I felt like I had the strength to do so was the moment she locked her pussy down on my dick, preventing movement. "Fuck!"

Chapter 34

TaNia

"This hotel too big," I mumbled as I walked swiftly in my Giuseppes. I really didn't plan on doing all this walking, because I would have grabbed some flats. I had to admit it: this was by far the nicest hotel I'd ever been in. It was an added bonus to have a free, all-access pass because I was in love with one of the owners. I was headed to check on him since Key said he was already drunk.

I laughed and shook my head as I pushed the button to call the elevator. I was about to step on when I saw two women come out of the bathroom, laughing.

"Girl, that motherfucker fucking the shit out of her. We could hear her ass through the walls," one of them said as the other kept laughing.

"Whoever the hell he is, I call next," she said as they disappeared into the crowd of people.

I turned back around when the doors to the elevator came open. I looked at them suspiciously as I weighed my options. I needed to go attend to Mon, but my nosy ass really wanted to know what was going on. I walked down the hallway that led to the restrooms and stopped short when I heard Mon's name being screamed on the other side of the door in the men's restroom.

"What the fuck?" I mumbled as I walked into the restroom, not caring that I was out of place. The sight before me literally broke my heart, spirit, and hope all at the same time. I couldn't move my feet as my heart began to race. I grabbed the wall beside me as my head started pounding as I watched one of Lemonte's waitresses on top of him, riding him as if she belonged there. Tears I couldn't prevent gathered in my eyes with every movement she made on top of him. I felt like I was about to throw up. "Lemonte," I mumbled, but they didn't hear me. That only made me more pissed. "Lemonte," I screamed with all the strength I had.

The bitch slowed her movements and looked back at me with a smirk on her face. "Lemonte," I said again, not knowing what else to do, but he didn't respond.

"He kind of busy with a real woman right now," the bitch said as she continued fucking him.

I launched at her, pulling her half-naked ass off him, and he still didn't move. "Bitch," I screamed as I repeatedly slammed my fist into her face. She tried fighting me off of her, but I was enraged. I heard her begging me to stop, but I couldn't. I kept hitting her and hitting her until I felt myself being pulled off of her. I looked down at what I had done and realized that she was unconscious.

"Let me go," I screamed as I fought against the person who held me.

"Calm down, little lady," he said, still holding me.

I looked over at the couch and saw Lemonte standing up, putting his pants back on. "Really, motherfucker?" I yelled at him. He looked up at me and smiled.

"I was waiting for you, baby," he said as he took a few steps toward us.

"Get your bitch off the floor," I yelled at Lemonte.

He shrugged his shoulders as he walked closer. "That ain't my bitch, but this is the men's restroom. What'chu doing in hurr?" he slurred.

I was waiting for him to get within reach so I could knock him out. Once he was, I grabbed as many of his dreads as I could and pulled him closer to me. With all the strength I had left I hit him, blow after blow until he grabbed me and stopped me.

"Yo, what the fuck?" he said in a confused tone. "My fucking head already pounding. Why the fuck would you hit me?"

"Fuck you," I screamed as I got away from the person holding me. "Don't touch me! Don't say shit to me! I fucking hate you, Lemonte," I cried as I stormed out the door. I heard him call my name, but I kept moving toward the front of the hotel as fast as I could.

Chapter 35

Winter

I was about to sneak up on Demarco as he talked to a guest when I was grabbed by my arm. I turned around and locked eyes with Reggie. He had a few of his friends with him, and I knew there was about to be some shit.

"Damn, Storm, you looking—"

"My name is Winter, Reginald," I said, intentionally using his government name. "What are you doing here?"

"Check it," he said, rubbing his hands together. "Me and my peoples got a suite tonight. We were looking for some entertainment, and I was trying to see if you were working tonight," he said as he grabbed a wad of money out of his pocket.

His homeboys were looking at me and licking their lips, and I immediately became uncomfortable. "Reggie—"

"What?" he asked, licking his lips at me. "You graduated now so you don't strip? Oh, wait. You got that fuck boy taking care of you?"

"Reggie, I don't want any trouble with you. Why don't you just go?"

He looked at me for a moment before he laughed. "Fuck that! I need a stripper for tonight, and you coming with me."

He went to grab my arm and was snatched back so quick that it made my head spin. I saw Demarco slam him to the ground with force, knocking all the wind out of his body. I let out a small scream when his homeboys rushed Demarco. They all rushed him, and I could only stand there and scream as Keyton ran over to help. The guests of the hotel all scattered from the lobby and started making their way to the stairs and elevators to get away from the commotion.

"Please," I heard one of the officers we had on duty yell. "Everyone clear the lobby. Please retreat to your rooms."

The guests continued to move up the stairs and up the elevator. Tori ran over to me with a confused look on her face. "What the hell happened?" she asked, grabbing me and pulling me back.

"Reggie ass came in here tripping," I yelled as Demarco landed a blow to Reggie that knocked him out. I was so scared he was going to kill him, and I didn't want him in jail for murder, so I pleaded for him to stop. "Please, Demarco, just let him go!"

He stopped what he was doing and let Reggie drop to the ground. He looked back at me with death in his eyes, a deep frown covering his attractive face. His dark blue suede Roberto Cavalli tuxedo was ripped as his chest rose and fell rapidly. I was so scared of what he would do. I didn't know if he thought I was talking to Reggie on a different level from what it was. The police finally got the guests out of the lobby and were picking Reggie and his crew up off the ground and helping them exit the building.

"I fucking swear, Winter," he said, pointing at me.

"I promise, baby, it wasn't like that," I immediately spoke.

"Fuck was the muthafucka in your face for?" he yelled, causing me to flinch.

Tears welled up in my eyes. "He said they got a suite and he wanted me to dance for them. I promise you, it wasn't what you think."

"Tell me what it was then," he yelled.

"Please, stop yelling, Demarco," I pleaded.

"Tell me what it was, Winter."

"I just told you," I cried. "He wanted me to dance."

He unbuttoned his jacket and ripped it off before tossing it at me. "That's what I get for being with a stripper, huh?"

The gasp from the people around us was deafening to my ears as I looked at him.

"What the fuck, Marco?" I heard Key say.

"That's messed up, Marco," Tori spoke softly.

I tried not to be embarrassed about my past because it was such a huge part of the person I was today. I didn't strip as a hobby. I stripped to make a way for myself. Were there other routes I could have taken? Yes, but I choose that lifestyle, and I guessed it was something that would haunt me for the rest of my life. I was both hurt and shocked to hear him say that to me. "Why would you say that to me?"

"It's true," he said as he removed his cufflinks. "Fucked up, ain't it?"

I let his jacket drop to the ground as I stepped closer to him. "Is that why you don't love me? You can't love a stripper, right? Just say it," I yelled, pushing his chest as my tears destroyed my makeup. "Say it," I screamed.

"Don't put your hands on me," he said, pushing me back.

"Fuck you," I cried as Keyton grabbed me before I could hit him. "I fucking hate you, Demarco. I regret the day I gave yo' weak ass five seconds!"

"You hate me," he asked as he grabbed me out of Keyton's arms. "You fucking hate me," he yelled as I swung and connected with his jaw. He let me go and grabbed me around my waist. "Don't fucking hit me!"

I broke free from him and turned around to face him. He looked at me as if he was confused.

I took deep breaths to calm myself down as Tori took steps toward me. I put my hand up to stop her. "Please, Tori, I promise I'm fine. I'm fucking great," I said, looking back at Demarco. "You don't have to worry about me ever fucking speaking to you again."

I turned to walk out of the hotel as I heard Key yelling TaNia's name. I didn't even look back. I just needed to get away from Demarco.

Chapter 36

Demarco

"What the fuck did I just do?" I mumbled as I watched a visually broken Winter walk out of the hotel. I looked back as I heard Mon calling TaNia, who was walking full speed with her arms crossed over her chest with tears falling down her face. Tori immediately walked over as they walked out of the hotel.

"Fuck you do?" Key said, snatching Mon up as he passed to follow TaNia.

Mon looked spaced out, as if there were nothing behind his eyes. I hardly recognized him. "I don't know," he mumbled. "My fucking head is banging."

"You look fucked up, Mon. What the hell happened?"

"Delia said some shit, did some shit. Then TaNia said some shit, did some shit," he said then laughed. "I can't remember."

Keyton ran a frustrated hand down his face as he looked between Mon and me. "Both you fools need to get y'all shit together. We can't be out here acting fucking crazy. This is our income. Our livelihood. We can't have a hotel no one wants to come to because the owners are crazy as hell," he said as he removed his jacket. "And you," he said, pointing at me. "That shit you said to Winter was wack as fuck."

"What the hell you do to Winter?" Mon asked.

"Nothing," I said as we walked to the front of the hotel where the ladies were. "I need to find her."

We all started walking toward the exit. When we got outside, the street was clear, and the nightfall was uneasy. Something didn't feel right. I looked down the block and saw Winter walking, the tail of her Cavalli ball gown dragging on the ground.

"She doesn't want to talk to you, asshole," Tori said, rolling her eyes with her hands on her hip. "That girl loves the hell out of you, and you too blind to appreciate her. She gon' find someone worth her time, and I'm gon' laugh in your face when she does."

"No, the fuck she not," I said as I turned to follow her. I heard TaNia and Key going at it as they faded into the background. "Winter!" I called out to her as she kept walking. "Bring your ass back here!"

"Fuck you," she yelled over her shoulder.

"Bring your stubborn ass back here," I laughed as she kept walking. Her ass jiggled in her dress. It wasn't helping the fact that I wanted her.

I broke out into a light jog as I heard tires screech on the street. I looked up in time to see an all-black Tahoe with dark tint hit the corner. The passenger windows came down, and two AK-47s hung out the window.

"Marco!" I heard Key yell. I knew what it was, but I had to get to Winter. I pulled my gun out my back and start busting before they did.

"Get down, Winter," I yelled as gunfire erupted. I saw Winter hit the ground, and I was just praying that she got down in time. I bear crawled to her as fast as I could as the air filled with smoke.

"Winter!" I yelled her name, and she didn't move. I felt my heart drop as my mind thought the worst. "Shit," I growled as I felt a bullet hit my thigh. But I kept moving.

When I finally made it to Winter, she was shaking, lying face down on the pavement. "No, no, no, no, man. God, please," I cried as I pulled her to me.

She had a bullet wound going through her stomach as blood spilled from her mouth. I pressed down on her stomach, putting on as much pressure as my shaking hands would allow as thoughts flooded my mind of losing the only thing that ever mattered to me. "Please, baby," I cried as she looked into my eyes. She tried to talk, but blood just spilled from her mouth. "Don't talk, ma. Just breathe. Just keep breathing, all right?"

"Help," I screamed up the sidewalk as I saw Keyton standing in the middle of downtown Dallas, busting back at the car that just shot at us.

I heard sirens in the distance as the footsteps came up behind us. "Oh, my God, Winter," TaNia cried with her nine in her hand.

"Call the police," I tried to speak as best I could.

"They coming, Winter. Please hold on," she cried as she ran back up the sidewalk.

Winter tried to talk again, and it just made me cry harder.

"Please, Winter. I'm sorry! I was so stupid," I cried as I buried my face in her neck. "I love you," I said the words that she wanted to hear, but I felt like it was too late. Blood covered her beautiful face, sliding down her cheek into her hair. Her all-white dress was now stained with her blood, which had also covered me. I felt like I was suffocating as I held her, rocking her in my arms with her body pressed against mine.

"Please, baby, I love you so much," I screamed into her neck. "Hold on, okay?" I spoke into her ear. "Say, you remember that time in your kitchen when you said that I didn't care about you before we left for Turks and Caicos?" I said as tears moved down my face. "I've loved you since the day I laid eyes on you. I just didn't know it. I just didn't know how to tell you. I love you, Winter. Please don't leave me."

I felt her body become weaker as her breathing slowed then eventually came to a stop.

"Winter!"

To be continued . . .

. . . in Relationship Status Book 2: Still Tied.

Relationship Status Book 2:

Still Tied

by

Deshon Dreamz

Chapter 1

Keyton

"You're bleeding," Tori screamed as she ran toward me. "You can't die, Key!"

Her overdramatic ass. "It's a flesh wound in my arm," I yelled, tucking my gun in the back of my slacks. "Get'cho ass back in the building, Tori! You, TaNia, and Winter go upstairs!"

"What if they come back? I can't find TaNia or Winter! Where are they? Where is Mon?"

I exhaled as I walked down the street, looking down the sidewalk, where I saw TaNia running toward us. She had a gun in her hand. I heard somebody bustin' back with me, and I just assumed it was Mon, but it was Nia.

She had tears coming down her face, even worse than before.

"What happened, TaNia?" Tori yelled as the ambulance and more police pulled up.

"It's Winter," TaNia sobbed. "She was hit! She needs help!"

"Fuck," I yelled as I ran down the sidewalk.

Demarco held Winter tight in his arms, rocking her. I never saw him cry, but he had a million tears falling from his eyes as he held her motionless body. He mumbled her name in her ear repeatedly as he continued rocking her. The EMT came and had to pry Winter out of his hands and place her on the stretcher.

"Go with them, Tori. Nia, get Mon and get him to the hospital. That nigga clearly out of it."

They both nodded as they took off to do what I asked. I turned to look down at Marco, who was zoned out and covered in blood.

"Marco, we have to get to the hospital with Winter! Come on," I said as I bent down to help him stand up.

He looked up at me as I pulled him up. "I fucked up, Key," he said slowly. "My nigga, I screwed up," he sobbed, holding on to me.

"We just have to get to Winter, Marco," I said, trying to keep my emotions together. I couldn't even look at Winter when they pulled her out of Marco's arms.

I knew he would be fucked up if he lost her. Sometimes it takes almost losing the thing that matters the most to you for you to appreciate it.

I knew that all too well. I looked Marco over to ensure that he wasn't hit, and that was when I noticed he was shot in the leg.

"Shit, Marco, we have to get you to the hospital."

"Fuck this leg, man. Just get me to Winter, Key. Please, dude, I have to make sure she is all right. I got to . . . Fuck, bruh. I gotta make sure she knows I love her."

I nodded my understanding as I threw his arm around my neck and started walking back up the sidewalk. I saw the ambulance rush off with Winter.

TaNia walked back out of the hotel and toward us, still visibly upset. "Mon is in the second ambulance about to leave. I'm going to ride with him. I have the police getting the car for you guys." Her voice trembled as she spoke.

I couldn't do anything but respect TaNia for stepping up and tending to shit like a boss. She was clearly shaken up by it all, but she was dealing with it. My respect for her was on a different level.

"I need to get to Winter," she cooed.

I grabbed her with my free arm. "We all do. Just go with Mon, and make sure he's good. We right behind y'all."

She nodded a few times before she turned and walked down to the ambulance and got in.

The officer I hired walked up to me. "Come on. You can bring him this way. Cortez has the car waiting."

"The lobby clear?" I asked him.

"Everyone was gone by the time the shooting started. Everyone else has cleared out. We're about to close everything down now."

"Once you do that, get to the hospital. Tell the other unit to stay here on watch."

"All right," he said, nodding. "Cortez has the car on the side of the building."

Once we got into the car, the silence around us pulled us all in. I was more concerned about Winter than anything else. She didn't look good when she left.

That shit came out of nowhere! I mean, here I was thinking we were being low-key with our movements and flying under the radar, but clearly, we had someone watching our movements very closely.

I looked down and grabbed my ringing phone out of my pocket. "Hello."

"Hello, Key?" Tori yelled in my ear.

"Yes, baby," I said as I moved the phone back from my ear. She was so loud.

"Oh, thank God," she sobbed in a quiet voice. "I'm so glad you're okay."

"Tori, it's a flesh wound."

"I know that, Key. I just saw blood everywhere, and I was so scared of losing you! I love you so much."

I grabbed my forehead and rubbed it. "I love you too, ma. We're pulling up at the hospital now. How is Winter?"

"They rushed her back to surgery. I just heard them say she had a light pulse when she got here. I am just praying that she is all right. I haven't known her long, but I love her. I'm so scared, Key."

I exhaled. "Don't worry, baby. She gon' be good."

"I called her parents, and they're on the way."

"Good," I said, jumping out of the truck and rushing inside the hospital. Marco, of course, led the way, walking as if he didn't have a bullet lodged in him. "Where you at, ma?"

"Right here," she said.

I turned around, and she was speed walking toward me. She wrapped her arms around my neck tight, almost to the point of suffocation, and sobbed into my neck.

"You all right, Tori?" I said, prying her off me so that I could look her over. Her light makeup was ruined, and her hair was out of place, but she was still breathtaking.

"I'm okay," she said in a rush before wrapping her arms back around me. She finally released me to look at my arm.

"Oh, my God," she exclaimed. "You need a doctor."

"Tori, calm down," I said, looking into her eyes. "It's a scratch, thank God. I'm going to be fine, maybe just some stitches."

She grabbed me again and wrapped her arms around me. "I was so scared. I'm still scared."

"It's all right, baby," I said, running my hands through her hair. "Everything is going to be all right."

I looked over and saw Marco pacing back and forth. I knew he was scaring the hell out of the people in the hospital, but no one was bold enough to say anything. I then saw Nia walking across to the sitting area.

"Do you know if she got Mon checked in, Tori?"

"She did, but something happened between them. She keeps crying and trying to leave. I don't know what's going on."

"Do me a favor, ma," I said, looking down at her. "Sit over there with Nia and try to calm her down. I don't know what happened between her and Mon, but she's fucked up about it. I need to check on Mon and give Marco the update on Winter."

She nodded as she kissed me before walking over to Nia. I looked their way for a minute, watching Nia as she placed her face in her hands and cried.

"What the fuck did Mon do?" I mumbled as I turned to walk over to Marco.

He stopped pacing when he saw me. "Yo, I'm about to go back there with Winter!"

"How?"

"I'm about to go get this bullet out of me. Once I'm done, I'm going to her room. If anyone asks, I'm her brother."

I figured he was about to say some shit like that. "Just stay calm, man. Her people on the way."

He rubbed his waves nervously. "Who called them?"

"Tori said she did."

"Damn, man. They gon' hate my ass, rightfully so."

"Just relax, bro. You didn't see that shit coming. I didn't even fucking see it."

"Yeah, and me slacking got my girl in there fighting for her life. I gotta see her."

"We gotta figure out how we gonna handle this shit! Apparently, they don't give a fuck about harming our girls because of whatever beef they got with us. Can't help but think this shit linked to Flacco, man. Remember the shit he sent them bitches to do to Tori?"

"But how do they even know that's my girl? They have to be fucking close to us, because we been under the radar. I'm starting to think it's a fucking snake in the camp."

His words made sense. I mean, for them to know Winter, for them to know the opening was tonight, for them to know all of our movements, the shit just didn't seem right.

"You go check on Winter. I'll check on Mon and tell everybody what we doing. We are moving the girls into the safe house, and keep the details on the families. I'm about to go talk to Tori and Nia now."

"All right, bro," Marco said as he walked off.

Once I saw him check in, I made my way over to Tori and TaNia. I saw the officer I hired standing not far from them. "Say, where the fuck Cortez at?"

He shook his head as he walked over to me. "I haven't seen him since we got here."

I nodded, letting that process. "Watch that nigga."

Chapter 2

Cortez

This shit was driving me crazy. All I wanted was her. Once I got her, I could leave town and never come back. I wondered what she would think if she knew how I felt about her. I mean, I loved her just as long as he did, if not longer. I would always sit back and watch her. After all, that was my job: to keep an eye on her every movement any time she was in my presence.

In doing my job, some might say that I developed an infatuation for her. I needed her to know how I felt, then maybe we could have left town together and never gone back to this hellhole. I was always on the fence about my involvement in this shit, but it wasn't about anyone else but her. I never wanted her to get hurt. If something were to happen to her and I knew I had anything to do with it, then taking a bullet to the dome would have been the only way for me to get over that shit. I just wanted her to know that I loved her. Maybe I did not have as much money as that punk-ass nigga, but I was getting my money right so that we could disappear.

I watched her as she walked over to the chair and sat down. She looked around and shook her head before she buried her face in her hands. I was pissed off because she wasn't happy, and it was all because of that nigga she was with. I was tired of that "if only" speech I would give myself every night. I was so ready to have her with me without any interruptions from the outside world. We were going to be good as fuck together as soon as I made my move.

She was talking to someone I couldn't see, and I knew it wasn't that nigga because his dumb ass was disposed of at the moment. Slipping some shit in his drink was easy enough. If only Delia's young, dumb, and full-of-cum ass would have followed through with the shit she was supposed to do, I would have my baby in my arms and move on from all this other shit. I just couldn't get her ass out of my system no matter what I tried or did.

I should've been got my ass out of here because I knew they would kill me the minute they found out how I was tied into this shit. Hurting her, though, that was never part of the plan, never. I would never be involved with anything that involved causing harm to her. I could not stay at this hospital, and I wanted to take her with me, but I knew that at this time she would not come. But I would be back for her.